The major novelist of the post 80's period, Pratibha is also a short story writer and literary activist. She has also written travelogues and essays. She has steered clear of the hapless alienated human situation to discover human greatness and feminine grace in the myths and legends of the great epics - Ramayana and Mahabharat. Her interests are multi-fold, from historical periods and myths to great monuments and figures as well as the dark realities of the Bonda tribal and other deprived segments of the society. Her range is vast and varied and her narratives are expressive, interpretive, argumentative and at times even magical.

– **Prafulla Kumar Mohanty**
Former Professor in English, Translator and Critic

Although Ray's locales vary with the story line and the inevitable denouement, there is always a discernibly unique thematic and narrative pattern in her fictional landscape. Whether it is "The Curse" or stories like "The Gentleman", "Hunger", "The Other God", "The Untouchable God" or "The Mango Tree", Ray excels in the leisurely unfolding of the drama of human emotions. In most of such tales, the actual "event", "happening" or plot plays a subordinate role. The focus of attention in most of these realistic works is not on the "happening" though there is the inevitable tour de force in many stories, as in the best of Chekhov or O Henry.

– **Sachidananda Mohanty**
Former Professor in English, Translator and Critic

TRANSGRESSION
AND OTHER STORIES

TRANSGRESSION
AND OTHER STORIES

Pratibha Ray

Edited by
Dr. Adyasha Das

BLACK EAGLE BOOKS
2020

BLACK EAGLE BOOKS

USA address:
7464 Wisdom Lane
Dublin, OH 43016

India address:
E/312, Trident Galaxy, Kalinga Nagar,
Bhubaneswar-751003, Odisha, India

E-mail: info@blackeaglebooks.org
Website: www.blackeaglebooks.org

First International Edition published by
BLACK EAGLE BOOKS, 2020

TRANSGRESSION AND OTHER STORIES
by **Pratibha Ray**

Edited by
Dr. Adyasha Das

Cover & Interior Design: Ezy's Publication

ISBN- 978-1-64560-075-6(Paperback)
Library of Congress Control Number: 2020938507

Printed in United States of America

Foreword

The evolution of Odia literature can be traced back to the writing of the Mahabharata by Sarala Das in the fifteenth century. Though Abadhuta Narayana Swamy's " Rudra Sudhanidhi", sixteenth century and Brajanath Badajena's "Chatura Binod", eighteenth century included folk-tales and narratives, it is Fakirmohan Senapati's creative endeavours that helped establish fiction as a significant literary form in Odia. The Odia short story has undergone significant transformations since Fakirmohan's "Rebati", published in 1898 and considered the first ever short story published in Odia language. Since then, it has led to the emergence of a steady stream of writers who persistently experiment with various techniques of narration and themes.

Pratibha Ray was born in a coastal village of Odisha in 1944, three years before National Independence and eight years after Odisha got her identity and political map, on the basis of language. This period is significant because Odisha was journeying towards revisiting her history, culture and language with her new born confidence. Women's education was in a primitive stage and higher education was centered around Ravenshaw

College, Cuttack; but Pratibha's visionary father Parashuram Das, himself the headmaster of a village school in Balikuda, wanted her talented daughter to launch her ambitions to reach starry heights.

Pratibha is a celebrated name in Indian fiction writing. Among the contemporary short story writers and novelists of Odisha, she is undoubtedly one of the most gifted and accomplished. She is the recipient of the prestigious Jnanpith award, the first and only female Odia writer to have received this highest literary recognition of India and the Padmashree, the fourth-highest civilian award in the Republic of India; she has received numerous awards including the Sarala Award and the Odisha and Central Sahitya Akademi Award. She received the Moorti Devi Award for her widely acclaimed novel Yajnaseni, the first and only female author to have been bestowed with this coveted recognition. She has been consistently crafting novels and short stories in her mother tongue Odia, since forty-five years. Her search for a "social order based on equality, love, peace and integration", continues in her creations since she first wrote at the age of nine.

Pratibha has textured a poetic and epistolary narratology in her fictions. Love of nature, culture and rituals, love of life and universal issues are powerful entities found in almost all her novels and stories. Despite her identity as a writer of novels, she is widely acclaimed as a powerful story teller. Her stories range from the quiet and profound experiences of life to middle class humdrum existence as well as universal concerns. In her creations, she expresses modernity through the prism of tradition, myth, folklore, legend and metaphors. Pratibha said in an interview, "In the Indian context, modernity and tradition coexist. They are not antithetical to each other."

Pratibha's short stories have a deep understanding of the human psyche. Some of her stories are socio-ethical, some are ritually mysterious and some are feministic in appeal. She has written more than 300 short stories and has about 26 story collections. She takes lesser known figures of everyday life to the larger scene and makes them heroic, sacrificial and grand. She however does not call her work 'history'; she fictionalises facts without the dispassionateness of a historian.

"Transgression and Other Stories" is a collection featuring fifteen representative stories of Pratibha translated into English. In these, she has skilfully used her varied life experiences to enrich her creations. Her style is brilliant and succinct yet leaning on a descriptive, symbolic use of language. Her short stories are defined by an interesting stream-of-consciousness style; an in-depth knowledge of language has influenced her unique vocabulary. In some of these stories, she explores the hidden recesses of the human mind and character, with a colloquial flavor and an eye for the odd detail that became the hall-mark of all her fictions, including the best of her tales.

Pratibha's short story and fictional world is not an imaginary landscape. It is embedded in a concrete socio-historical reality and Odisha's rich cultural heritage. Her forte lies in her ability to employ the traditional mode of narration to depict the changing pattern of Odisha's primarily rural culture. The story "Animal Birth " uses a powerful tribal setting as its backdrop, another area where Pratibha has worked extensively.

Pratibha's locales differ in keeping with the story line and the inevitable denouement but there is invariably a noticeably unique thematic and narrative pattern in her creative landscape. In her story "The Curse" or "The Gentleman", "Hunger", "The Other God", "The Untouchable God" or "The Mango Tree", she deftly crafts the leisurely flow of a canopy of human emotions. In many of her tales, the actual "event", "occurrence" or plot is relegated to the background. The attention in these realistic portrayals is not on the "happening" though, as in the best of Chekhov or O Henry, there is the inevitable tour de force."

Ray's stories are relentless in their indictment of social discrimination and injustice. Prejudice and obscurantism of all kinds are her particular bête-noir as in "The Other God", a story that is a fierce critique of the supposedly "civilized" behavior of man. In this story and the very moving "The Untouchable God", she deftly reveals the evil of blind religiosity that ignores human fellowship. Many of the tales seem to question the claims of tradition and authority. In her stories, such interrogation often leads her to question patriarchal modes of conduct and belief. A noticeable pro-woman attitude has been variedly manifestated in stories such as "Salvation" where a couple Shoshi and Nuri Das live together under one roof for forty long years, yet neither speaks nor sees each other's face. Expressed through the use of masterly irony, "The Curse" depicts a complex trade-off between the need for sexual identity and social respectability. Pratibha's women are illustrative of what she herself has said in several interviews, a sort of "humanist feminism" without the rigour or rancor of a Julia Kristeva or Luce Irrigaray.

In her tales, Pratibha seems to prefer the dissidents, the drop-outs or the odd ball rather than heroes and heroines in the classic sense of the term. Her stories suggest a constant spirit of questioning and search for the meaning of life. She celebrates the life of the sense and emotions that inevitably bring to mind D.H.Lawrence's "You touched me" or "The Horse Dealer's Daughter". It is through such myriad gestures that Pratibha's characters break out of the prison-house of the self and live a life of fulfillment.

Many of the stories in this collection have a rural setting made fragrant by the aroma of fields and arbours. Human relationship is her central focus in the stories. Love, friendship, fellow feeling and other subtle nuances of social life are examined with tender sympathy and respect. Pratibha's stories elevate humans above the sickening confrontations with the dark forces that lurk in men and women. She makes her people real and surreal but does not portray evil. Classical values and human dignity enrich her stories. She brings out the best in her men and women in all testing circumstances. She however, does not idealize or idolize, she does not sacrifice reality for abstract values.

Pratibha, as a story teller inhabits a world which is solid, holistic and suffused with different colours of life. She believes that man's divinity is a gift of nature, the essence of creation, and this essence could be polished by the challenging vicissitudes of life so that mankind can make the world their rightful home. She visualizes human reality in the multiplex context of the mundane, the sophisticated and the divine. Her characters are identifiably real and the use of sensuous and symbolic metaphors makes her men and women palpable and perfectly human despite their angularities and naiveté. Pratibha is definitely one of the most important story tellers in contemporary Indian Literature.

Among the stories included in this collection, Pratibha has received New Delhi's prestigious Katha award for "The Ketaki Grove" and "The Curse", and the Sahitya Akademi award for "Transgression". "Salvation" received the best regional feature film award from Government of India as well as the best film story award by Government of Odisha. Surfing between tradition and modernity, Pratibha Ray's short story collection Transgression and Other Stories hopscotches between pathos and poignant reflections to make it a stimulating collection.

Dr. Adyasha Das

Contents

The pages are still blank, but there is a miraculous feeling of the words being there, written in invisible ink and clamoring to become visible.

- Vladimir Nabokov

The Blanket

Translated by **Jayanta Mahapatra**

That was mother's-in-law memento. She used it those last few days before her death. Her son, Manmath, had bought the blanket with his scholarship money and had given it to her as a present while he was studying in college years ago. The blanket had been folded carefully with mothballs placed between layers. Then, it had been wrapped in a much-washed white sari and stored in an old trunk. Even during the cold winters, the blanket never saw the light of day. In the exotic aroma of mothballs, huddled against a corner of the trunk, the blanket reposed sleepily, savouring the warmth of the trunk's inside. Mother-in-law would go through even the most bone-chilling of winters with her hand-sewn, patched old cotton sheets, but she would never dream of taking out that costly foreign blanket of hers. Her younger cousin would at times taunt her with, "Don't be so stingy, Sister! Do you think Manmath will not buy you a more expensive blanket when he gets a job? Is that why you hold on to this one? Can't you foresee what

Manmath will grow up to be? The first leaf of a basil plant has an aroma. If he could get you an English blanket while he was studying, can there be any doubt that he'll bring you a silver-embroidered one when he starts working?"

Nirmala would then, in a gesture of reverence, put both her palms together and look up at the skies. In a voice tinged with melancholy, she'd say, "Is he man as yet that I should think of such things? Let the gods grant him a long life, let him grow up to be a man first."

And Sebati would counter, "Oh yes, but you know how severe the winter is this year. The English blanket should be just right. A blanket is meant for the winter chill. Did Manu bring it all the way from Cuttack so you could stack it up somewhere?"

Nirmala would open the trunk. She'd lift the blanket with great care, as though it were a sleeping child. As though she were afraid the child would awaken and cry out in distress. How touchy and churlish her Manu had been when he was a child! Even today when he came home on a holiday, he behaved in more or less the same irascible manner. Nirmala would let her hands move softly over the layers of the folded blanket, feeling it tenderly, caressingly. As if it's small, warm sleep would be upset were she rough with it! Then, with a shy smile, she'd gingerly, slowly, stroke its silk binding and announce with pride, "Sebati! Have you noticed how exquisitely the border has been done! Look at the way the strands of silk have been woven together — like a garland of jasmine buds, or a row of chubby children playing leap-frog. Whichever way you look at it, it is ingeniously beautiful! Look at its colour. How soft and sleek it is, with the flushed hues of an onion skin, as though it would leave a mark if you simply touched it. Have you seen another like this, where the rose tint of the body complements exactly the mauve of the intricate silk binding? Really, I can't stand those other blankets — hairy, shaggy things that only chafe the skin!" She grimaced and went on, 'and if you pull one of those over your body, how suffocated you get! To top it all, the awful smell. As though it were bear or sheep skin! But this one — this has a baby-skin scent. Perhaps it is the only one of its kind. Look everywhere, I'm sure you won't see one half as good in the whole village! Take my word, there's no one to surpass my son Manu when it comes to choosing something. His choice is absolutely the best!"

And Sebati would quip with an amused smile about her lips, "Ah, Sister! You speak as if Manu had woven the blanket himself," and burst into laughter.

Nirmala would put the blanket back carefully in its place. "Will such a thing ever be available again?" she'd ask. "My son bought it with his scholarship money, for me to remember all my life. If I use it, it will surely be spoiled and torn in the long run. After all, what good does an English blanket do in the penetrating cold around here? One needs quilts, the warmth of a fire. When my Manu becomes a man, I'll ask him to buy me a quilt. A quilt is said to be warmer, cozier. Yes, I'll have one made for my later days."

Indeed, Nirmala had never used a quilt in her life. Who did in those days? Especially for a woman, a quilt was unheard of. Usually old, worn-thin saris were pressed together and stitched one over the other to make a thick, flat sheet. It was an art, making those, and one lasted an entire lifetime. Winter never came to a standstill for the lack of a quilt or a blanket. Nirmala was truly adept at stitching these sheets for she could also embroider pretty designs on them—parakeets and elephants, pitchers and lotuses and the sun. And new clothes slowly became old, and when the old sheets tore, they were replaced by newer ones. Every year after the long rains, Nirmala's blanket stole its warmth from the sun, silently through the hours. Winter came and went, not caring for blankets or quilts or old sheets, and, with the passage of time, Nirmala became a mother-in-law at last.

Mira came to the house as the daughter-in-law. As usual, Nirmala took out her old clothes along with her precious blanket to be aired in the autumn sun. Mira helped her mother-in-law to spread them in the courtyard. Mira's gaze fell upon the onion-hued fleecy blanket and froze. As, wide-eyed, she watched her mother-in-law gently unfold the blanket and flatten it out, the wonder was unmistakable in Mira's eyes. Even though she tried her best to hide her feelings, her covetousness seemed to break through the evening sky of her eyes, like shimmering stars. Strange, but this blanket seemed totally out of place among the assorted clothes in the trunk! How could such a fabulous imported blanket come to be in the possession of her mother-in-law?

Nirmala asked Mira to hold on to one edge of the blanket while she kept brushing the other end, and began passionately, "You know, Manu bought this with his scholarship money. It is seven years old already, and I haven't ever used it. Day by day, the blanket seems to look brighter, doesn't it? Anyone who sees it is fascinated by it. Is there another like it? Manu, too, was such a delightful child that passers-by would stop and stare at him. I haven't seen another child with the looks Manu had as a baby. With all his studying, and now with this responsible post which makes him travel the year round, he's really lost those looks. What was the necessity, after all, of taking this important job? Where does he get time to settle down, relax a little, and have a single meal in peace? You know how his father left us homeless all of a sudden. But Manu studied brilliantly, got a scholarship, and climbed from rung to rung. And now he doesn't get an hour to rest."

Eyes flushed with tears, Nirmala hung the blanket up with painstaking care and caressed it with her palm. She gently brushed off an almost invisible speck of dirt, imagining perhaps that she was wiping the drops of sweat on Manmath's tired forehead.

Mira found it hard to appreciate Nirmala's sentiments. She could merely stare at the blanket and think, what good is such a blanket if it is merely stored away in some old trunk? Even if her mother-in-law covered herself with it, who would realize the value of such a blanket in a remote village? How would this blanket look beside the patched-up sheets on Nirmala's old-fashioned rosewood bed? On the other hand, such a blanket would adorn a modern bedroom, would enhance its looks. People would notice it, know it was a foreign one, and talk about its unique colour and workmanship. Why, she had never seen anything resembling this in her life! The newly-wedded Mira had begun to think highly of her husband's tastes.

But the next moment she couldn't see the sense of it all, of a gift that was given away by her husband without thought. Was it appropriate to have presented his mother with such a blanket? A hand-woven sari or images of Lord Jagannath, perhaps an appliqué canopy from Pipili that she could place over the gods in her prayer room, could easily have satisfied her. And since he had decided on a blanket, couldn't he have chosen a more usable one? His mother might then have put it to proper daily use. He could have kept this blanket for himself!

Mira was straightening out the folds in the blanket when she said, "What good is it if you put away such a marvelous thing inside a trunk? Only if you use it, will it be noticed, talked about. Why don't you use it this winter? It will be ideal for the chill. This will never chafe your skin so silken and smooth. Really I've never seen one like this."

Nirmala was ecstatic. "You haven't seen one, have you? I knew it! Like Manu, this one has no parallel in the world. That is exactly why I lay it aside in mothballs. Can you ever replace it?"

Mira's outburst was spontaneous. "Better things than this are available today. Will this blanket wear away so soon? Can't we get another for you if it tears?"

Nirmala brushed the blanket tenderly with her palm once again. Her throat felt a little constricted. In a voice thick with emotion, she said, "Yes, you'll get everything. But then you won't be able to buy one with Manu's scholarship money, will you? Can't you just get me a quilt for my use right now?"

Mira said eagerly, "A quilt isn't a big thing. If you don't want to use this blanket, please use the quilt that I brought along in my trousseau."

Mira had a feeling that her mother-in-law would give her the blanket in exchange for the quilt. For surely Nirmala would consider her daughter-in-law to be the fittest person for the use of her blanket. A quilt, Mira thought, could be procured at any time.

But it would never be possible to buy a blanket exactly like this one; a better one, maybe, but not one like her mother's-in-law.

Mira's heart fell when she saw her mother-in-law carefully fold the blanket. She heard her say, "But why should you part with your quilt? My days have gone with these cotton sheets. If you could make me a quilt, it should last until my death. Isn't a quilt warmer? For whether the heart wants it or not, this aging body longs for a little comfort. But I want to keep my blanket as it is. Such a blanket was never meant to be used; you know. Besides, your children will see it someday and understand that their father studied on a scholarship."

Nirmala pushed the mothballs between the folds, wrapped the blanket in an old white sari, locked it in her trunk—and thus shut the door on the secret hopes of Mira's.

Even after settling down in another town with her husband, Mira vividly remembered the affair of the blanket. There always lurked in her heart some unfulfilled need, even in the midst of the luxuries with which she had surrounded herself. She even bought a couple of imported blankets. Nevertheless, it was hard to shake that old feeling off; as though there really had been only one such blanket made in the whole world, just as her mother-in-law had insisted. At times, she would needle her husband, "Why does your mother store that blanket of hers? She should be using it at her age. It's truly a marvelous thing! One could never get another like it to day!"

Manmath would respond with a broad grin, "That's why I gave it to her. Isn't it fabulous? I once thought that all the world's beautiful things were made for my mother alone! Who else was there but Mother for me to think of?", and he would give Mira an amused smile.

Once Manmath asked his mother, "Why do you lay the blanket aside, Mother? Don't you feel chill in these old cotton sheets of yours? Your son holds a good job now, but you never let go of your old things!"

Nirmala smiled and answered, "Do the days stop moving because of this? Do you remember how you'd curl your skinny body against mine and snuggle into the warmth of these sheets — all those years till you passed your high school exams?"

And Manmath thought to himself, truly what comforting days those were! Of course, the chill seeped in through the flimsy cottons. If he had been somewhat careless in his sleep, his body would have turned into ice. But he would pull the sheet off his mother's body in his sleep and lie till dawn in restful warmth. When he awoke, he would feel guilty for having used the sheet himself while he let his mother shiver through the night. He would tell himself to be more careful in future. But, strangely, the same thing happened every night. It was only much later Manmath realized that it was his mother who covered him up to ward off the cold. His tender heart went out to his mother for her concern. He promised himself he would buy her a really good blanket when he got his scholarship money. Manmath kept his word. But his mother treasured the blanket in her old trunk. Manmath told himself it was hers, so she could do with it what she wished.

Nirmala noticed her son's serious demeanour. True, her daughter-in-law had advised her often to use the blanket. But how could they understand that such a blanket was not meant to be used by a common villager. Had he forgotten, too, that he had bought it with his scholarship money? If they wanted to, they could buy her a quilt, which she would use until her death.

Manmath said somewhat absent-mindedly, "Well, if you wish, we'll have a quilt made for you next year."

He instructed Mira to send her a quilt next year before the winter.

Mira answered, "I've thought so too. But it slips my mind. We'll send her one next year."

But when the mild breezes of spring begin to blow, one forgets the chill of the winter months. In the heat of the scorching summer, one literally begins to pine for the cool touch of winter. Effortlessly, today's matters are lost when tomorrow comes; and every year, when the chill became severe, Mira recalled that a quilt had to be made for her mother-in-law. But by then the winter had half gone. Had she ordered one then, it would have taken not less than three weeks for the quilt to be delivered. It would be best if the quilt were sent to her next year before the advent of winter, so she'd be able to use it for the entire season.

So, each year around the middle of winter, Mira or Manmath would remember the quilt they had promised Nirmala. Each accused the other for being negligent. Their plans for the quilt were left for the following year. Gradually, Mira consoled herself with the thought that the quilt was not that essential for her mother-in-law. Otherwise, wouldn't she herself have reminded Mira about it? Then, one day, some thought made Manmath exclaim, "Oh, let it be! If the winter is that severe, Mother has her blanket to cover herself with. What use is a quilt when the night is drawing to a close?"

In reality, Manmath sensed that his mother was nearing her end. Mira felt that too. Manmath and his wife brought the old lady from her village so she'd be with them when the end came. Nirmala had not forgotten to pack her blanket along with her other belongings when she left her village. How could she have parted with it in those final days, when she had lavished such motherly care on it through the years?

Nirmala often shivered from the fever that attacked her. She suffered from the extreme cold that seemed to enter her bones. Her patched-up cotton sheets were useless. One day, Manmath took the blanket out of Normal's trunk and covered her frail and trembling body. "Why do you treasure it, Mother?" he asked. "You never used it even for a day." His voice was choked with emotion. A mist formed in front of his eyes. Eagerly, Nirmala pulled the blanket close to her and answered, "If you feel unhappy, my son, then here you are. I'll use it from now on until my death. But you are here beside me. What harm is there if the blanket goes with me to the burning ground? Let all your ills, troubles, and dangers rest in this blanket. Let them be mine. I have prayed for this all my life. Let God be your refuge from this moment on. It's time for me to rest."

Nirmala closed her eyes and let the warm caress of the blanket seep into her aching bones. Calm entered her heart, and she asked herself, who said a quilt was more comfortable? If I'd known earlier that Manu's blanket would be so warm, I would have used it long ago. But I feel my winter is coming to its end. From her closed eyelids two tears silently trickled down her cheeks in contentment perhaps or in pain.

Mira felt satisfied that her mother-in-law had, at last, made use of the blanket; but for how long? The doctor had predicted fifteen days, or a month at the most. Everyone admired the blanket Nirmala used, and friends and relatives were convinced that the son and daughter-in-law had not ill-treated her. Mira recalled how her mother-in-law had spoken of the blanket being taken to the burning ground. For according to ritual, all the dead person's possessions—mattress, pillow, and sheets were taken by the dhobi before the pyre was lit. Would such a remarkable blanket end this way? The thought totally upset Mira. The impending loss of the blanket was greater torment indeed than the death of Nirmala. No one could go against the laws of the world, but one could certainly prevent the blanket's falling into strange hands.

A solution occurred to Mira at last. She reasoned that there was no harm in it. She pulled a clean white cover over her own quilt and covered Nirmala with it when she was asleep. She removed the English blanket. Let the quilt go with the dhobi, she told herself. Making another was no problem at all. But to replace this matchless blanket was quite impossible!

Nirmala awakened from sleep with a start. The first thing she noticed was the missing blanket. Distraught, she began to rave, "My blanket! Where's my blanket?"

Mira caressed her mother-in-law's feet. "So often you have asked us for a quilt. But we haven't been able to make you one through sheer negligence. This one is my own. Your English blanket will not be enough to suppress your shivers and keep you warm. So I have stored it away carefully in your trunk."

Nirmala asked, "Where's Manu?"

"He's here in the house. He took leave from the office because you're ill. He doesn't go out of the house," Mira explained indulgently.

Nirmala felt relieved. She went on weakly, "Well, if Manu is here, why I need the blanket? Let it be where it is. But what will you do in this winter chill? You gave away your own quilt just because I asked you for one long ago!" The old woman's voice sounded worried.

Mira's answer came through faintly. "The winter is almost over. I can manage somehow. But you need the quilt more than we do now, what with spasms that keep racking your body!"

Nirmala stretched out her hand and fondly patted Mira's cheek. Blessings seemed to pour forth from her weakened eyes. "How very thoughtful you are, my child. Your goodness of heart will never go unrewarded. God will bless you always."

Tears shone in Nirmala's eyes. Inside her feverish palm, Mira's hand was bathed in sweat. It seemed to be growing weaker.

That night, Manmath wanted to know why Mira had given away her quilt. She repeated the words she had said earlier to her mother-in-law. But her voice was barely audible as she spoke, the words unclear. Somehow all her excitement about the blanket had diminished. One single thought kept fouling her mind—that she had lied to her mother-in-law while she lay on her deathbed, that she had succumbed to the temptation of a mere blanket! Mira had received all her blessings from that simple, truthful heart, despite her own deceitful words.

Nirmala's life came to an end few days later. She used the quilt until her death. She would point to the quilt when relatives came to visit her and say, "A present from my daughter-in-law! Who knows what she is using herself in this chill! What a generous, thoughtful girl, my Mira!", and there was praise for Mira all around.

The blanket was totally Mira's after the old lady's death. Mira had at first wanted to place it in her bedroom, where it would look grand. But strangely, she, like Nirmala, aired the blanket in the sun, packed it with mothballs, and stored it away on the lowest shelf of her cupboard. Manmath laughed at her actions. "Women are all of the same mind. You were the one to accuse Mother! For whom do you treasure it now? Mother laid it aside all these years, and whom does it serve now?"

Mira's voice grew soft, trembled. "Well, that's all we have left of Mother." Mira's eyes clouded with tears. Manmath was amazed by his wife's esteem for his mother; why, he had never had an inkling of it when she was alive! How little he actually knew of Mira, he thought, even though he had been living with her all these years!

At times, he told her, "If you would use that blanket, Mira, I'd sleep better perhaps."

"Why?" Mira asked, and Manmath answered, "Even though Mother used it for just few days, every strand of it exudes the scent of her body. When it's aired in the sun, the unmistakable scent is everywhere. One doesn't feel she is dead, but is here, moving around the house. If you use it beside me at night, Mother's presence will put me to sleep. Somehow, with increasing age, I haven't been able to get to sleep lately."

Mira tried often to use the blanket. She tried to erase certain thoughts from her mind. But when her eyes closed, the blanket's weight lay heavy upon her chest. A choking sensation gripped her at times. The words of her mother-in-law as she lay close to death, like a benediction, became more oppressive and burdensome with the days. She thought, a simple deceit, a single lie I uttered once—for that, do I have to pay such a terrible penalty? Why hadn't she thought of that before? Now it wasn't easy to express her agony before her husband or children, or even her friends. Her unspoken anguish began to torment her. How petty she would appear was this to be known! All the years she had nursed her mother-in-law would vanish into nothingness at the admission of that single lie. She could imagine people pointing their fingers at her, saying what a small mind she had; to have pulled a mere imported blanket off her mother's-in-law wasted body! How the dying woman had to bear the harsh winter with a torn old quilt!

When the blanket was aired in the sun, the neighbours admired it and spoke of its exceptional quality. And Mira remarked with a dismal look in her eyes, "That's the only memory of Mother we have." But her throat dried up, her vision blurred. They withdrew, talking of Mira's love and re-spect for the dead lady. But Mira's heart cringed inside in her grief.

In time, Mira's repressed sorrow increased even further. Then, one day, she fell ill with a high fever. Her fever continued and she began to shiver. Her body slowly weakened. The doctor failed to diagnose her malady. The blood tests showed nothing wrong. One day Manmath came home early and found her lying nearly unconscious. He felt her forehead, found it was burning. Her feet were clammy and cold to his touch. She trembled a little in her sleep. He thought she might be feeling a chill. The thick winter quilts were in locked trunks in the storage room, so he took his mother's blanket off its shelf in the cupboard and covered Mira with it. He had a feeling that his mother's blessing would soon see Mira to recovery. Mira slept on for a long time. When she awoke and noticed her mother's-in-law blanket on her body, she began to scream. She flung the blanket to the floor. Her body shook. "How did this blanket get here? Who covered me with it?" she cried. Manmath saw the look in Mira's eyes and suddenly felt afraid. Perhaps her fever had shot up, perhaps she was hallucinating. Gently, he sat her down. He picked the blanket up from the floor. His voice was soothing. "You were shivering from the cold. There was nothing else I could find. I thought that if I covered you up with Mother's blanket, you'd get well soon. Why are you upset about this?"

Mira's voice was unsteady. "Please, for God's sake, don't ever cover me with that blanket."

But why?" Manmath's surprised voice echoed in her ears.

"That is all we have of Mother, that memento," she mumbled. "With what care she preserved it all those years." Tears started flowing from Mira's eyes. She could not restrain them. But she could not say anything. Manmath's eyes brimmed too as the memories flooded in, feeling the love and regard he perceived in Mira's heart at the moment. He held her close and added, "Let it be as you say. We'll keep the blanket with care. If you'd like to keep Mother's memory alive, why should I destroy it?" A moment later he said, "Mira dear, how generous you are! Really, how much you have cared for my mother!"

Mira's eyes grew hazy again with tears. She said incoherently, "Oh, don't ever say that please. It pains me a lot. Please. Wasn't she my mother as well?"

Manmath sat, overwhelmed by Mira's words. Mira felt she would rot inside in agony. How could she get a little peace? How could she free herself from this torment once and for all?

When one takes a nap on a winter afternoon, a chill seems to envelop the body. Mira's fever had persisted through many days; it had not ever completely left her. She suffered from shivers in her bones whenever she rested, especially during the afternoon, when the thought of the blanket, it would bear down upon her as a load on her mind. She'd think of her mother-in-law and the graces she had showered on Mira, and her mind would turn to her own deceit—to be swallowed up again, in unbearable agony. One day Mira grew restless. She suddenly seemed to hear someone's call, poignant and faint, outside the house. Must be the beggar woman, she thought. Mira usually felt irritated when she heard the old woman's voice. But on this afternoon, she walked up to the verandah and asked, "What is it you want? Haven't I told you often that there would be no rice left if you came this late in the afternoon?"

The old woman said piteously, "I'm not begging for a bowl of rice today. But if you could kindly give me something to cover myself with, something torn and old, anything you have, God will bless you, my daughter. The old man will not last long in this chill. One can live without food for three days, but this merciless cold will not let us survive. It turns the bones to ice." She dabbed at her eyes. "If you won't let me have something, the old man will surely never live through this night. And he's had a fever for the past four days."

Mira simply stood there, motionless, for a long while. She didn't know what to say. Could the old man possibly survive with a thin cotton sheet? Mira turned round abruptly and went in, opened her cupboard, and brought out her precious blanket. With firm steps, she walked to the front gate and placed the blanket in the old woman's outstretched hands. Her heart seemed to open out, expand. Her voice was husky when she said, "Here, this is my mother-in-law's memento. I am not being generous. But if you are going to bless me, say a prayer for my mother-in-law, that she may rest in peace."

The beggar woman was stunned. She couldn't believe her eyes. Was this real or all a dream? In a frightened voice, she pleaded, "I am a mere beggar. What will I do with such a thing? I wanted only a torn, tattered sheet."

Mira was firm. "I cannot take back what I've given you already. It is a blanket. Do use it. I am sure your old man will recover. Take it and go your way."

Manmath had just come back from his office. The disbelief in his voice was obvious. "What have you done, Mira? Our only memento of Mother - and you gave it away! You could have given something else. But to hand over Mother's memory... I find it hard to understand you."

Mira asked the beggar woman to leave and shut the gate. She walked into the house ahead of Manmath. Without looking at him, she said, "It's our only memento of Mother, but it doesn't necessarily mean that it should be kept under lock and key. I think I've used Mother's memory in the best possible way. Every year, do you remember, Mother used to give away her hand-sewn cotton sheets and old clothes to the poor? I gave the blanket away so that Mother's soul would rest in peace. I feel certain that the woman's blessings will fall on her in that other world..."

Manmath reached for her hand. He touched her forehead and said excitedly, "You don't have a fever today. Mira I feel so relieved."

The intense tone of Mira's voice softened Manmath, "No, I don't have fever. But there's a pain inside me, a pain that persists somewhere."

Manmath's heart melted in sympathy. He said, "But the doctor insisted there was nothing wrong with you. If one could only look into the heart..."

Pale, he began searching for the pain in Mira's heart.

■

Adoration

Translated by **Bikram Das**

The Ramayan tells us that when Ram went into exile in the forest, his younger brother Bharat begged him for his sandals, which he placed on the throne and worshipped in token of his devotion. No one has matched Bharat for piety, but Bidhan's devotion to his uncle reminded many of the Ramayan. Some, however, considered it a mere show. Adoration of one's parents one could understand, but an uncle? There was not even a photograph of Bidhan's parents in the house, let alone their sandals, but the uncle's sandals were being worshipped!

When his children questioned him he explained "When my father passed away I was just a boy, studying in the ninth class. It was my uncle who brought me up. I can't remember my father ever holding me in his lap when he was alive, he was so strict ! So I was closer to my uncle."

He knew this wasn't a satisfactory reply to his children's questions, but could he tell them everything ? And even if he did, would they be able to understand ?

His worship of his uncle's sandals was widely talked about among friends and relations. Not that he wanted to make it public ; on the contrary, the sandals had been kept in a corner, on an old piece of red velvet that was spread over the little wooden throne on which the deities were placed . The sandalwood paste that he had smeared over them had dried up. Each year, on his uncle's death anniversary, he worshipped the footwear with sandalwood paste and incense. Being only a nephew and not a son, he was not entitled to make the ritual offering to his uncle's soul. Each day, however, after his bath, he bowed to the images of the gods and the memory of his parents and aunt. And to his uncle's sandals. That was all, but it could not remain a secret. These days, grown-up sons neglected their parents even when they were living ; who had heard of a nephew showing so much regard for a dead uncle ? It was an example to others. "Go and have a look at Bidhan," friends and relations would tell their children. "How learned he is, how respected ! And yet he worships his uncle's sandals ! It's his devotion to ancestors that brings him heaven's blessings! Can't you learn from him ?"

When someone praised Bidhan to his face he would shrink with humility. Some unknown sorrow raked his heart. He could see his uncle's feeble feet, tired from eighty years of walking. His eyes would grow moist. Why did people take so much interest in the affairs of others ? Why open old wounds ? Wasn't it one's personal choice whom one would worship? Why should others talk ?

When he told his own children about the family set up he had grown up in, they didn't believe him. Or if they did, they didn't approve. More like a herd of cattle. My God ! Grandfather, grandmother, father, elder and younger uncles and their wives, visiting uncles and aunts-in-law, cousins ; everyone's children. House servants, farm labourers. All eating together. The fire in the hearth never grew cold. How could they all have lived together, keeping their mouths shut, like dumb cattle, with all individual desires, tastes, preferences forgotten ?

The children dressed in identical clothes. The women were

divided into those whose husbands were living and those whose husbands were dead ; all were dressed in the same coarse saris, except that the widows wore white. Of course, the saris which came as gifts from parents could differ – but there was no ban on women borrowing each other's clothes or ornaments. It was more a crowd than a home. The constant chatter. Each person busy, but no one resentful of the work. Someone engaged in cutting up vegetables, another in fetching water. Work was passed happily from one hand to another, like an infant being passed from one lap to the next. If the women had dissensions among themselves, the men never knew. They lived in separate kingdoms. Young Bidhan was acquainted with the events in the men's kingdom, but like his father and uncle, he knew nothing of the other world. His father was stern, hard-working and honest to a fault. Bidhan never ventured near him. Neither did his father ever display any tenderness for his children. Only, when he sometimes went to Cuttack to attend to his duties in the court, he would bring back an earthen pot full of the rasagollas for which Kandharpur was famous, to be shared by all. Bidhan loved rasagollas. In fact, the rapidly growing child loved all good things. Each member of the family would get one, but there were two rasagollas for each child. His father kept count while ordering the sweets ! But Bidhan had never seen his own mother or aunt ever eat a rasagolla. His mother would force his grandmother to have her share because, after all, old people had to be pampered, like children. Bidhan invariably got his uncle's share as well. His uncle would call him to the backyard and put the rasagolla in his mouth. "Eat it up quickly," he would say, "If that swarm of locusts see you, they will pounce on you." Bidhan would gobble up the sweet quickly, thinking " My uncle could have given the rasagolla to his own son Biraj ! " Bidhan was known for his healthy appetite but that was no reason why a nephew should be treated differently from a son.

His uncle was neither as intelligent nor as hard-working as his father. He had tried his hand at a dozen trades and failed at each. A lot of his father's money was sacrificed in the attempts to set his uncle up. Gradually, he came to be counted among the worthless. He looked after the family's agricultural lands. In a joint family no one starved because he was out of work. But Bidhan never thought of his uncle as useless. He was probably the most hard-working member of the family. Bidhan's aunt had charge of the family kitchen and spent much of her life there. When everyone had been fed and the vessels washed and put away, it was midnight. His aunt's weak back would have given way by then. She was unable to get up in the morning. He had often seen his uncle massaging her legs or rubbing ointment into her back. Only useless men who were slaves to their wives were supposed to do such things. But Bidhan knew this was not true of his uncle, or else the foundations of that vast family would have been shaken. Who would have looked after his poor aunt if not his uncle ? When she had finished all her chores, she would massage the legs of Bidhan's mother. But he had never seen his mother lay a hand on his aunt's aching body. How could she ? The aunt was her junior in the family hierarchy ! Bidhan's mother did not share the heavy work ; being the eldest brother's wife, all she was expected to do was to order people around, with the bunch of keys tied to the end of her sari. The younger brother's wife had to remain in attendance at all times ; that was the unwritten rule in a joint family. But the aunt lacked neither food nor clothing. Her children and those of Bidhan's mother were treated exactly alike. The two women ate out of the same bronze dish. As his aunt had some trouble in getting up in the morning, Bidhan's uncle would go to the kitchen and make a potful of tea, which he served to everyone, servants included. Then he prepared breakfast for the children. Milk and green leaves were boiled and vegetables fried for the women to eat with their pakhala (rice soaked in water and curd). The aunt bathed late in the morning, when the sun was warm overhead, to avoid getting a backache. How could she to go to the kitchen before her bath ? The uncle might be considered useless, but being a male, he was allowed to go to the kitchen unwashed. He was an expert cook. When there was a marriage in the family, he would prepare an array of pithas, rice-cakes and other sweetmeats. Even the aunt was not as skilled in the kitchen as Bidhan's uncle. While preparing tea for the others he would gulp down several cups himself and chew a few mouthfuls of chooda, flattened rice; that was his breakfast. Since he ate so little, he was rather sickly. He made sure that all the children in that vast family had their morning bath, were properly dressed and sent off to school ; those too young to go to school were carried around in his lap. There were about five women in the family, but their only responsibility was to produce a child each year. Bringing up the child would be no problem.

Bidhan's uncle spent the afternoons overseeing the family lands. In the evenings he would gather the children together and tell them stories, so that no child could doze off before the evening meal had been cooked. He also had to look after visiting relatives, manage the family thakurbari (temple), make sure the cattle were fed and the cattle-shed cleaned. No other member of the family went near the cow-shed, though everyone enjoyed a share of the milk, curds and ghee. When the ponds had to be cleaned or coconuts plucked from the trees, it was the uncle who looked after everything. But none of these chores were supposed to be a man's job If one didn't earn money from work, of what use was it ? It was only the women who worked for nothing ! Bidhan's uncle received no credit for all the work that he did. His father was respected by all as the family head, but whether this respect was given because he was the eldest son or because he was in a government job was difficult to tell. The uncle was only a grown-up dependent, whom the family had to shelter ! If the family lands were ever partitioned, the produce from the uncle's share would have been greater than that from his father's share – but in the eyes of everyone, the uncle was only the family retainer ! But he had no regrets. That too was part of the joint family code.

His uncle loved children. The children swarmed around him like pigeons roosting on the dome of a temple. There were always a couple of them riding on his shoulders. His favourite, however, was Bidhan . That was because Bidhan seemed the only hope in that crowd of idlers.

In the constant hubbub and confusion of a joint family, no

one paid any attention to studies – neither the children nor their elders. Just as a cowherd boy was appointed to keep watch over the cattle, so too was a 'tuition master', a failed matriculate, appointed to keep watch over the herd of children. He looked after their studies only in name. His real job was to be witness to the endless battles in which they were embroiled. The children had to be stopped from bathing in the pond too long, so there was the master with his stick. When eating, they had to be told not to leave any rice in their plates, so there was the master with his stick. In the summer afternoons they were supposed to sleep indoors and not run around in the heat, so there was the master with his stick ; while playing together in the evenings, they had to be prevented from smashing each other's heads, so there was the master with his stick. There was never a piece of chalk in the master's hands, only the stick. Who else but the poor master could control the little monsters ? Even the parents would call out to him when their children needed disciplining "Master, come here ! Give this rascal a stroke !"

It was, in fact, Bidhan's uncle who managed the children and attended to all their problems, and not once did he so much as raise a finger at them. Perhaps that was why all four of his sons turned vagabonds. But Bidhan was different, from the earliest days. Quiet and well-behaved, he never neglected his studies. The master's stick had never touched him. Always the first boy in the class. And so he was as dear to his uncle as the string of tulsi beads around his neck. It was always "Bidhan, Bidhan !" Bidhan first and his own son Biraj afterwards. If it had been the other way around, people might have accused him of being partial ; but since it was always Bidhan first, people said he was like a god. Biraj was always getting scolded while Bidhan was praised. He must have resented it, and that was probably why he turned vagabond.

That year, Bidhan was to appear at the Middle School examination. He would be awarded a scholarship if he did well. But the examination was being held at the Haripur High School, five miles away. How would he get there ? There were no cars or buses then, and his uncle had never learnt to ride a bicycle. His father could ride a bicycle, but he had the court work to attend to.

" No problem, " his uncle said. " He can't walk to Haripur, he's far too weak for that, but I'll carry him on my shoulders." It wasn't just on the few days of the examination that he carried Bidhan ; it was for a whole month, for he had asked one of the teachers in the school to coach Bidhan for the examination. It was high summer, and the sandy village road was hot enough to blister the feet. The journey must have been painful because Bidhan's uncle never used any footwear, like most people in the village. If anyone had worn footwear, he would have been accused of being a fop ! The family could have afforded a pair of sandals for Bidhan's uncle, but no one thought it necessary.

Bidhan rode to school on his uncle's shoulders, his head protected by an umbrella. His uncle tottered slowly across the burning sand. By the time they reached Haripur, he could barely stand. He would sit resting on the school verandah until Bidhan's studies were done ; then he would buy some snacks for Bidhan and a tumblerful of tea for himself.

When returning home with Bidhan on his shoulders his uncle would ask " Are you comfortable, son ?" "Why shouldn't I be ?" Bidhan would reply. "You are doing all the walking while I ride comfortably on your shoulders !"

" Yes, but you have to study and use your brains, " his uncle said. " That's the most painful thing of all. Don't I see how much strain your father has to suffer ? And what is it I do ? Just take the occasional walk, eat and sleep ! Nothing painful about that at all."

" But your feet must be hurting, Uncle," Bidhan said.

His uncle would grin and say " Well, it's just for a few days. Your exams will be over soon, and then you'll get a scholarship and a seat in the hostel and come to Haripur to study. And one day you'll become a big officer in the government and bring honour to the family. "

"But Uncle," Bidhan would say in a tearful voice, " I can't bear to see those blisters on your feet."

" Well, don't let that bother you, silly boy ! You'll buy me a pair of sandals when you are in a big job, won't you ?"

"If I buy you a pair of sandals will you wear them ?" Bidhan asked.

" I'll not only wear them, I'll walk all over the village in them and show them to everyone" his uncle replied.

Bidhan had won a scholarship. What a sensation that created in the little village ! One day, the barber asked Bidhan's father, while giving him a massage "Sir, we hear your nephew has got a scholarship. You must be very happy."

"What do you mean, nephew ?" Bidhan's father shouted, getting up and giving him a hearty slap. "Don't you know Bidhan is my son ?"

"We thought he was your nephew because it is the Younger Master (Bidhan's uncle) who always carries him around on his shoulders," the barber said apologetically.

"What difference does that make ?" Bidhan's father said. " Is a nephew different from a son ? I don't have the time to carry him around, that's all."

When Bidhan's uncle heard of the incident he had a good laugh. "When Bidhan was born, his mother nearly died," he explained. " Elder Brother brought the baby to my wife and said 'I don't think she is going to survive. From this day, you must look after this child as your own.' Well, Elder Sister-in-law did survive, but I have always thought of him as my own son."

Long after the death of Bidhan's father, his uncle still remembered the incident. "Today Bidhan is a big officer, earning thousands of rupees a month, but Elder Brother is not there to see it. " Bidhan's father had passed away at the age of fifty-two, which was a critical time for him astrologically. Bidhan was only twelve or thirteen then. He had had to stand on his own two feet and depend on his intelligence and determination to take him to the top. But could he say that he owed nothing to his uncle ? True, he had been on scholarships throughout his student career, but would that have sufficed to meet all his needs ? It was his uncle who carried rice, ghee, jaggery and coconuts from the village to the hostel where Behan lived. Even after he had started working, the supply of provisions from the village had never ceased. Bidhan

Babu's regard for his uncle had never diminished either ; he sent sweets from the town and medicines for his uncle's asthma. That was enough to keep his uncle in bliss.

The years had passed and Bidhan had grown old, while his uncle had become an ancient, doddering wreck. He could no longer come to the city. His sons and daughters-in-law did not give him the care that could have been expected. Who needs a helpless old couple in the house ? Bidhan too was enmeshed in his own worries; being in service, he was transferred frequently from one place to another. It was difficult enough to move around with his wife and children ; how could he have carried the ancient couple with him ? His uncle and aunt were unwilling to move from the village to the city .His uncle was an invalid now; his asthma had grown worse. A ripe mango, waiting to drop. Bidhan visited the village sometimes, carrying sweets, but could never spend more than a day or two there. His uncle was sinking fast. Neighbours and relatives came to see him, certain that the end was near. When Bidhan Babu got the news, he too went, with a pot of rasagollas from Kandharpur.

" Is there anything you wish for ?" relatives asked the old man. " If there is, tell your nephew. He will get it for you. He's a rich man now ; he has come in his own car."

"Nephew ? What do you mean, nephew ? Bidhan is my son!"

" Very well, he's your son," Bidhan's aunt said. " Tell him if there's anything you wish to have."

"Wish ?" the old man said. " Yes, I do have a wish – I've had it for years. I would like to wear a pair of sandals, like the ones Elder Brother wore when he went to the court. Bidhan had told me he would get me a pair. That was long ago. He must have forgotten. "

When Bidhan heard these words he felt as though his insides were being ripped apart. It wasn't as though he had forgotten about the sandals – how could he ? But perhaps he hadn't taken the old man seriously enough, thinking that he had merely been playing children's games with him. If his uncle had really wanted a pair of sandals, why hadn't he been told ? There were so many things that his aunt would ask him for when he returned to the village – a woolen shawl, medicines, an umbrella ... But who had ever mentioned the sandals ? Maybe his uncle had hesitated to ask ... after all, Bidhan was only a nephew. It would have been different with a son. Bidhan had, in fact, thought of getting the sandals once or twice. But then he had thought, would his uncle really use them ? Where could he go in those sandals ? Did Bidhan too think, like the others, that his uncle didn't deserve a pair of sandals, since he did no work?

Bidhan returned to the city, a sad man. But that day he bought a pair of sandals for his uncle.

On his next visit, Bidhan slipped the sandals on his uncle's battered feet and was rewarded by a glimmer in the old man's eyes. His grandchildren burst out laughing, saying "Grandfather can walk to the court now ... "

Fortunately, the old man had lost his hearing. But some of the women did smile, keeping their lips pressed together. Someone whispered "The old man wants to pamper himself now, when he is at death's door !"

Bidhan was bowed down by remorse. Why had he staged this farce ? It was obvious that he had bought the sandals only to rid himself of guilt, not out of concern for his uncle.

Bidhan's uncle departed. The sandals lay close to his feet. Till the moment of death, he kept saying " Leave them on my feet ; Bidhan got them for me. I will walk again soon !" The will to live grew stronger as the end drew near, but the pair of sandals was not powerful enough to halt death's chariot.

After his uncle had been cremated, Bidhan carried the pair of sandals home as a relic. His uncle's feet had touched them only once.

Ram had promised to Bharat that he would return after fourteen years of exile. Bidhan's uncle had given him no such promise, but at the height of summer, when the earth turned into a burning griddle, Bidhan could feel the tramp of his uncle's sandal-clad feet across his chest.

Salvation

Translated by **Sachidananda Mohanty**

Imagine a man and a woman living "together" under the same roof. For forty long years they share joy and sorrow. Yet, they neither speak nor see each other's face, let alone touch each other.

Forty –five years after Shoshi stepped into Nuri Das's house, she was dead. As Satia, the notorious son of Nuri Das (popularly known as the 'liar') kindled the mouth of the corpse with ceremonial fire, Nuri Das looked straight at her face.

Shoshi's face appeared rather hazy to Nuri Das, for by that time, his eyes had developed cataract. At fifty-nine, he was not exactly young. A streak of the noon day sun appearing from behind a puff of cotton-wool clouds lit up Shoshi's face of full fifty-eight years. It was as though someone from the depth of the sky had flashed a torch before Satia could accomplish his task. Despite the extra illumination, it was hard for Nuri Das to make out Shoshi's face. There was only a vague impression. How could this help one imagine the face as it must have looked forty-five years back? As it is, custom forbade Nuri Das to see the face of Shoshi after her death.

Cremation over, Nuri Das returned home and experienced an acute sense of loneliness. It was hard for him to enter the courtyard where for forty-five years he had observed the movement of Shoshi's feet. Nor could he sit on the verandah where Shoshi used to serve food twice a day. Instead, he went and sat at the feet of the aged mango tree in the garden in front. Why is he missing her so much? What, after all, did he share with her, he wondered.

The sight of Shoshi's face was enough to make Nuri Das turn away; just as he had done for years at the sight of the hands carrying rice in the brass bowls. When Nuri Das spoke to the wall or the fence, there was always a reply from Shoshi. Somehow, she seemed to always know his requirements. Therefore, there seldom was a need to call her. Shoshi would place things before him as and when required. At daybreak, red tea made up of jaggery along with fried rice. Then four pieces of betel leaf. When Nuri Das was finished, there was an assortment of garden equipment laid out before him: spade, hoe, buckets, basket and others.

The work in the garden began. Later, the smell of the curry cooked by Shoshi would remind him of the passage of the sun and the arrival of noon. Time to break! Before Nuri Das set foot in the house, he would be greeted by a bottle of oil in the front verandah. A quick dip in the garden pond, his well-oiled body would emerge to find everything laid out for his prayer. Sitting cross-legged, Nuri Das drew lines of sandalwood paste on his arm and forehead till the tip of the nose. He would plant a circular spot in between the two lines of sandalwood paste and draw a line on his chest. By the time he lifted his head after bowing to God, lunch was there already laid out for him. He would sit down, and like a good boy, eat without a complaint. There was, of course, no way Shoshi could know what he thought of her cooking. She managed to get an idea when occasionally Nuri Das asked for a second helping of rice.

Great care and caution marked Shoshi's cooking for Nuri

Das. Shoshi could very well realize that it was sheer bad luck that the poor man could not speak to her. She knew that he was perfectly capable of sensing both hunger and anger. For, none but Shoshi knew how carefully a man like Nuri Das lived his life.

Although Nuri Das never had a proper look at Shoshi, she must have peered at him from beneath the veil of her saree. Himself, he remained the same as he used to be in his youth-neither lost nor gained weight. Age was perhaps the only change visible in him. From being erect, he now looked somewhat bent. There is a certain charm and manliness at different stages of our life. In this Nuri Das had not suffered an iota of loss. With a spotlessly white dhoti above his knee, at home he was bare bodied; a white shirt when he set out to the market, the only dress he had. Both indoor and outdoor, he sported a red towel along with a garland of tulsi beads around his neck. To put it in rustic language, he would be described as a man measuring "five hands". He was of a dark complexion but looked handsome with a straight nose, broad forehead, small but sharp eyes, chest wide like a doorframe, shoulders tall and straight like a ploughshare. Still his stomach always receded inside. It was as if he never ate enough. But both his hands and feet were strong. Even without touching him, you could easily see how sturdy they were; enough to indicate that though poor, he had the figure of a real male.

Barring a tiny plot in the backyard with its modest crop, Nuri Das possessed no landed property. Apart from two or three mango trees, drumstick, banana and jack fruit trees, basically he ran the house by growing and selling seasonal fruits and vegetables in the market. There was, however, good income during the mango season. Nuri Das had no idea of the parentage of that particular mango tree. It bore a special variety: big, round shaped and juicy, a mango with a very thin skin, ideal to cut and eat! One's whole body, from the stomach upwards would be filled with its flavour. Nuri Das could easily quote the price by just looking at the mango.

The family of three survived on this tiny vegetable garden. Inside, there was a little pond where one bathed. There was irrigation round the year. During summer, when the pond dried up, one managed by digging a pit inside it. Like the stars in the sky, Nuri Das' pond got filled with fish of many kinds. They were of little use to Nuri Das since he was a Vaishnav, and a complete vegetarian at that. There was a prohibition of fish and meat at home. He allowed neighbours to catch fish but everything else in his backyard was out of bounds for them.

Summer came as a dry and lean season with very little vegetable. For one who lived by the sale of vegetables, such a season could not be more unwelcome for Nuri Das.

There was, however, another source of earning for Nuri Das. What began as a hobby was soon turned by the hunger at home into a necessity. During rituals and festivals, Nuri Das received gifts of polished rice, coconut, broken rice, sweets, money, clothes and towels. He was also fond of kirtan, singing devotional songs, a habit of long ago. Late in the evening, sitting in his dark verandah till the curry was ready, Nuri Das would play the Drum. At such times, the sound of the drum was low. But as night grew, midnight approached and Nuri Das' empty stomach turned, the notes became more sharp and insistent.

Many different kinds of hungers exist in this world. Just like the various tastes-sweet, sour, salty, hot and bitter. Their experience is also different. Hunger of the body, of the stomach, of the mind and of the soul-these are the four basic hungers. Many offshoots of these hungers cripple life of the creatures and trap it like a cobweb.

There are two hungers that Nuri Das recognized. For the hunger of the stomach, there was food, and as for the soul? Well, there was "Kirtan". The drumbeats of Nuri Das managed to merge the hunger of the body and mind with that of the soul.

It was hard to say whether Shoshi had any hunger of the stomach. Her hunger remained hidden behind her veil. All that Nuri Das could see were her two feet and hands.

From morning till evening she was constantly on the move. She made cow dung cakes, swept the house, cooked her meals, and washed her utensils. Not just the hunger of the stomach but the hunger of her body and mind got trodden along with cow dung under her feet. Who knows whether Shoshi's hunger of the soul gave company to Nuri Das' Kirtan and drumbeats.

In youth, Shoshi's feet were fair and slim. When she grew older, they swelled due to filaria. The top of her feet bore a patch of black, tattooed flowers. Her hands were soft and slim, the palms slender and delicate. Other than these, Shoshi's figure was totally unknown to Nuri Das. At times while serving rice, her uncovered arm came into view; an intricate spectacle of tattooed design! From within the veil, appeared a portion of her nose. No, not quite the nose, but only the nose ring of gold was visible. Those who had long association with Shoshi had never seen her saree ever slipping from her figure. In any case, none had ever seen Nuri Das' eye catch such a stray act. Needless to say, both of them were equally controlled and respectable. A real devotion to society's norms and ways!

If Shoshi's sister Shashi, younger to her by two years had not died of labour pain, after giving birth to a son of her in-laws' house, Shoshi wouldn't have had the ordeal of facing her whole life by concealing her face behind the veil. Shashi's husband Nuri Das, who was one among the five brothers, had come in adoption to his uncle's place that was bereft of children. Soon after this, his aunt became the mother of three children. Nuri Das predictably suffered the negligence of being an adopted son. But where could he go? As an adopted son, he had perhaps nurtured the hope that he would inherit the property of his uncle. After his father's death, his four brothers managed to make a living through the shares of their father's property. How could he return and claim his share? Did he not have his own self-respect?

It was around this time that Shashi's father was looking for a Ghar Jamai (a bridegroom who lives with his in-laws) for Shashi. By then of course, Shoshi had become a child-widow. Nuri Das left his uncle's place and came to his in-laws as a Ghar Jamai, a son-in-law who lives with his in-laws.

All went well till the first delivery of Shashi. Shashi's father too left this world after sighting the face of his grandson. It was left to Shoshi to adopt the little Satia. At home remained Nuri Das, a youth of twenty-nine years, Satia the son and Shoshi, the child-widow of eighteen years. Nuri Das would have got married again if only he had not been a Ghar Jamai . And he would have married Shoshi if only she had not been his wife's elder sister. Shoshi, after all, was only two years older than Shashi and younger than Nuri Das by eleven years.

The relationship between the two was pure as the water of the Ganges. It was strictly forbidden for them to see and talk to each other. Between them, there was no question of jokes and pranks. Despite many opportunities, the norms did not permit them to carry on such a relationship. It was, they knew, a sure invitation to hell.

After the death of her younger sister, through the neighborhood aunt, Shoshi had informed her sister's husband that if he wished he could return home, get married and raise a family. At his age, it's not the social norm for a male to remain single. However, Satia would remain here at her aunt's. He would perform funeral rituals for his family. He would not like to invite the shadow of his stepmother. Whenever Nuri Das wished, he could visit his son, but he ought to know that there was no question of taking him away.

It was of course not the intention of Nuri Das to spend the rest of his life as a celibate by cherishing the memory of Shashi. But the situation did not favour him with any definite foothold in either of the families. Could he return to his uncle's family and demand a share from his uncle's son? Who would grant him anything, even if he were to ask? Moreover, did he not have anything like self-respect? Could he continue to beg favours from so many households? Besides, Shoshi was younger by eleven years and a helpless child widow and Satia – a totally vulnerable kid.

Nuri Das said : "My father-in-law's property doesn't interest me. I only care for my son. There should be no talk of a second marriage in this house." That evening, Nuri Das removed his drum from the nail in the wall. The drum had accompanied him to the in-laws' house. At his uncle's house, along with his uncle, he was in the habit of doing Kirtan. The drum had lain unused for long in his in-laws' house. Today, it constituted his prized possession and was an intimate companion. That day he beat the drum hard till midnight. Soon after coming to this house as Shashi's husband, somehow he had forgotten about the drum.

As the saying goes: "Look at a cat if you haven't seen a tiger, look at your aunt if you haven't seen your mother." This was actually Satia's fate. Even now if he wished, Satia could see the tiger in the jungle or in a circus. But his mother he could not, for she was no more. Satia had seen the picture of the tiger but never had a chance to see his mother's picture. Everyone said that Satia's aunt gave him more love than a mother. However, since Satia had neither seen nor felt the mother's love, how could he differentiate his aunt's love from his mother's? Somehow, ever since he became conscious, Satia had become an impish liar.

Satia nursed complaints about his father because his father would call him maa khia (literally, eater of one's mother). In turn Satia would retaliate by calling his father maipa khia (eater of one's wife). This was of course not Satia's own coinage. The neighbours addressed Nuri Das as such. Where a girl of thirteen or fourteen would deliver, how could a sixteen-year old Shashi die of labour pain? Nuri Das' horoscope had indicated an evil omen for his wife. This had also been confirmed by many astrologers after the death of Satia's mother.

Nuri Das' house lay practically alongside the wall of the village high school set up during the time of the British. It was like having your meal at home and rinsing your mouth in the school. Nuri Das had thought that Satia , the maa khia, would pass his matriculation from the high school and would be treated as an educated man. He would earn his livelihood by taking up a government job. He would not have the insecure life of his father and not depend on the mangoes and the ritual offerings.

But somehow Satia became unmindful of his studies. The very thought of the school utterly scared him. Not only that, the father and the son seldom reached any agreement, and there were also frequent discords between the two. For days together Satia absented himself from the school and wandered around. At times, upon getting a complaint from the teacher, Nuri Das would tie up Satia inside the home. He would lock up the door from outside and say: "As long as he does not agree to go regularly to the school, none in this house will feed him." The last sentence was obviously meant for Shoshi. After all, barring Shoshi, who else in the house lived and cared for Satia!

Shoshi never replied back. For, wasn't the father pulling up the son for his own good? As an aunt, Shoshi had resolved to do her own duty. She was not prepared to allow anyone to thwart her. After Nuri Das left, Shoshi would open the door with the spare key. She would release Satia who was tied to the legs of the cot, then feed him after giving him a piece of her mind. When Nuri Das returned from the market, Satia would be holding a book like a good boy. Nuri Das would watch him without uttering a word. It's almost as if he knew this beforehand. Satia would have eaten rice, wiped away his tears, got freed and would be sitting with books. Beyond that it hardly mattered whether he studied or not.

Such would be the ritual. At least ten times every month. It was Satia's fate to be detained in every class for at least two to three years. Of course, this was not a matter of worry for Shoshi. If a good student who studied under a teacher's guidance passed and a spoilt one failed, then that's no credit to the teacher. After all, what kind of teacher is he, if he can't reform a wayward pupil?

Nuri Das found fault with Satia, Shoshi accused the teacher. Satia in turn held the father responsible. It seemed as if Satia was taking out his grudge against his father for having eaten up his mother. He would certainly pass if only he cared to study. But that alas would make his father feel happy whereas his real intention was the very opposite. No one could guess how the days of Nuri Das and Shoshi passed worrying over Satia. One day, the eighteen year old Satia left home, went to town and luckily managed to procure a job. At home remained only two beings: Nuri Das and Shoshi. There was no longer any need to worry over Satia: It's their own welfare they had to think of. Shoshi remained her crying self and Nuri Das remained sturdy and manly.

There was no fear of illness – only the pang of hunger remained. Other worries, if there were, must have lurked only in the mind, neither visible nor heard outside. Everything got muffled under the drumbeats of Nuri Das, all concealed under the veil of Shoshi.

In a village, the communities of milkmen, washer men and the Mohantys – all harbour their own share of shame involving forbidden liaisons in the joint family.

Perhaps the colourless austerity of village life needs its own bit of sensational diversion. The city dwellers get their own thrill through dance, cinema and the theatre. Where would you find such outlets in the village? From the bathing and washing ghat, verandah, panchayat office, news become sensations, sensations turning into full-fledged scandals. The result? Fines, social ostracism and exile from the village. And the solutions? Well, black magic, murder and suicide.

Nuri Das' household was, however, immune to all these. Only when Satia was around, was Nuri Das' house an object of curiosity. Assaults, court cases, abduction, all centered on Satia. The day Satia left the village, got married and moved to the town, Nuri Das' house became a closed soundless temple, attracting no attention of the passers – by. Of course, the villagers never gave any medals to Nuri Das or Shoshi for their firm moral and chaste behaviour. Carrying the burden of this world, Nuri Das and Shoshi gradually put on years.

Nuri Das' kirtans resulted in the disease of the lung, and Shoshi's increasing filaria to swollen feet. There was no way by which mutual help was possible. When Nuri Das suffered from asthma, all that Shoshi could do was to show sympathy from beneath the veil. And when Shoshi collapsed from filaria, Nuri Das could only sit on the verandah, facing the breeze and gently beat the drum. What else could be done? At times, the drumbeats resounded in their minds. Who had ordained that even to put water into the mouth of the one by the other would be treated as improper? It seemed perfectly all right for a sister-in-law to bear an illegitimate child, but massaging the feet of a filaria patient was a grave crime! Nuri Das' drum continued its loud beats.

The older the two grew, the fonder did they become of each other. The sorrow, pain and suffering of the one inevitably caused worry in the other. Although they never called out to each other openly, they had begun to address one another endearingly as "the old man "and "the old woman". For instance, in the female circle, Shoshi would say, "How the old man suffers! Asthma has completely ruined him! Not even a kitten at home to apply mustard oil! For the love of his son, he hanged around the in-laws' and spent his entire youth! Where are his son and daughter-in –law now? As long as I am alive, I shall continue to boil some rice for him. And after I go? What will the old man do? The fact is he is missing his son a lot. After all, he is part of his blood. I can well understand his grief without his having to tell me!"

Similarly, in the company of the males, Nuri Das would remark; "The old woman is down by filarial fever. There's none to put a drop of water into her mouth. Poor woman! She had love for the nephew more than a mother had. The blighter never treated her as his mother! Let's see whether he would come to perform the funeral rites. At least, that is the final wish of the old woman. She has not stated it. But I know it for sure!"

How did Nuri Das known of something which Shoshi had not said. This is a question no one bothered to ask. So much in the relationship among human beings remains unsaid but perhaps not unknown. Only the foolish think that the mouth is the only source of speech. One's hand and feet can also speak. Whether you like or dislike someone can be found out by your behavior, just as from your style of serving food, one can make out whether you are serving with care or not. From the drumbeat, one can know whether you are happy or sad. Your style of drawing water from the field can reveal whether your mind is insipid or laden with emotions. As it happens, the joy, sorrow, hunger, scarcity, worry, anxiety, anger, depression, understanding, and misunderstanding of forty-five long years have all got lost in two sealed mouths. It was never given to the one to call the other and say: "Here take half of my joy or share in my sorrow". Like the fragrance of the flowers getting lost in the wind, like the rain waters soaking the cracked earth, like the drumbeats smearing the moon, the feelings among human beings get shared spontaneously." That is why when Shoshi was down, Nuri Das gave up his ego and wrote a letter to Satia

Dear beloved Satyanand.

Your aunt is now in her death bed. Even though she has not said so, it is clear that she would like to see you at least once before she leaves this world. Moreover, she thinks that she will not get salvation unless you light the funeral fire. It's all right if you don't come in future. But for once do consider this letter as a wire and come immediately.

Ever your well-wisher

Nuri Das.

Satia knew that Nuri Das had retained his ego and written the letter on behalf of his aunt. That is why he had not signed "your father" at the end. Nevertheless, Satia left everything and came back immediately with his family. Not because of his father's request; it was only for the salvation of his aunt. He brought biscuits, fruits and sweets. By the time Satia reached home, Shoshi's final hour had come. Fortunately her eyes were semi-open, and there was a faint breathing. Whether Satia had come with alacrity or not, Shoshi had no way of finding out. But Satia knew that his aunt's soul had been yearning for him all the while. Before dawn broke the next day, Shoshi was gone.

Cremation over, Nuri Das returned and sitting with his eyes closed in the darkness of the verandah, he played his plaintive notes; Hare Krishna, Hare Rama, Krishna, Krishna Hare, Hare – Hare Hare, Rama Rama Hare Hare.

From inside was heard the lamentation of the daughter- in –law: "Oh dear aunt! Where have you gone leaving us!"

This was apparently a custom to propitiate the evil being.

Sitting beside the blown out oven, like a child Satia shed tears: "Oh Aunt, oh aunt!" As if his cries would let Shoshi attain salvation from aunt hood.

Throughout the night, the drum beat its mournful tunes.

The blood from the cracked tips of Nuri Das' fingers flowed and merged into his tune of salvation.

***

(In some parts of India, it is customary not to touch and see the face of the elder sister of one's wife. It is a taboo which is observed religiously even today.)

◼

The Stigma

Translated by **K.K. Mohapatra,**
Leelawati Mohapatra and **Sudhansu Mohanty**

Sarami was seized with a shameful bout of hysteria yet again. She clenched her fists, flung her legs obscenely about, rolled her head and yanked out her hair, shook her body and stuck out her tongue, brushed her sari off her breasts. One moment she laid limp, exhausted, her eyes closed and the next she was up, fiercely rolling her eyes, hissing like a snake and frothing at the mouth. It took four or five stout young fellows to restrain her. Alternately she laughed like a shameless hussy and wept like a wretched waif; sad like a silent grey afternoon one minute and riotous like a crazy sunset the next. Then the spell was over just as suddenly as it had begun.

Except for these periodic bouts, Sarami was every inch the typical shy bride, sensitive like a mimosa creeper. She never revealed herself, neither her moon-like face from behind her veil, nor her mind. The ankle chains she wore on her reddened feet tinkled ever so faintly when she tiptoed around. She was so gentle, so serene, so unruffled that she often resembled a sculpted image. It was of course quite another matter that despite her damnedest efforts to smother her youthful figure under layers of clothes, her voluptuousness was apparent. Her brother-in-law devoured her with his eyes; even Sudam, the young unmarried nephew of her husband unabashedly ogled her, mentally mapping her exciting contours. When a flower blooms in somebody's garden, it belongs to the garden owner but don't others get to feast their eyes on it and inhale its fragrance? The same held true for Sarami: she might have been Raghu Tiadi's wife but there was no earthly reason why others could not appreciate her or flirt with her a little. It was accepted social behaviour that a young brother-in-law could banter and take some verbal liberties with the new bride in the house. Even if Raghu Tiadi didn't like the idea, he would have to put up with it. To think that in the beginning he had even tried to shield his wife from Sudam, his nephew, the orphan of his own elder brother! Hadn't he brought him up since he was a little boy? If Raghu's first wife had borne him a son instead of a daughter the son would have been the same age as Sudam! What evil stars! The wife passed away in childbirth and the girl grew up, got married and had three girls herself. It had dealt a blow to Raghu's pride to be a grandfather to not one but three young girls. His second wife was a shade better: she bore three sons, but God alone knows what sins she had committed that she and her sons should have died when the evil goddess of smallpox visited the family. Sudam's father too fell to the scourge. Raghu's stars were bright, maybe he had the benefit of accumulated merit from previous births; he managed to claw back from the jaws of death, though losing an eye and developing a game-leg in the process. And of course plenty of tell-tale pockmarks on his handsome face. Young Sudam and his mother were away at his maternal uncle's place, and had thus escaped unscathed. The mother had lived a long life and had died only two years ago.

True, Raghu Tiadi had lost an eye and his good looks, as well as his erect gait, but he had not altogether been robbed of his manhood. He had the grave responsibility of preserving the family line from extinction. Sudam, already on the threshold of adulthood, could have been trusted to keep the line alive but Raghu Tiadi couldn't bear the thought that his name would be completely wiped out. No wonder he had seriously toyed with the idea of a third marriage. His well-wishers too had egged him on, and a search was mounted to hunt for young brides for both the uncle and the nephew. Regardless of the difference in age both wanted young girls and nubile young things were not exactly in short supply. But there weren't many from respectable, well-to-do families. And what did sweet sixteen's from poor family's amount to – nothing! Sudam had made it clear that he had no qualms about tying the knot with a girl short on looks but long on dowry. Paragons of virtue and beauty from humble homes could try their luck elsewhere. Why take on the eminently avoidable responsibility of providing food, clothing, jewellery, children and conjugal bliss to a girl from a poor family! There was only one way out for a good looking girl from a poor family: she could escape the curse of spinsterhood by hoping to be accepted as a second or third wife of some doddering old man.

When the matchmakers brought a proposal for Sarami, both Sudam and Raghu Tiadi went to inspect the prospective bride. Sudam took a shine to the girl but not to her father, who was as poor as a church mouse. Flowers and fruit were all such a man could offer as dowry. Agree to the match? No way. The girl had great looks, but so what? Her father didn't have enough money, he could never come to the son-in-law's rescue in his hour of need, and what's a father-in-law if he couldn't do that? Neither Sudam nor his uncle could give the go-ahead.

Sarami's father, who was blessed with not one but three millstones around his neck (grown girls were proverbially worse than fire, one never knew when they'd burn the good name of the family to cinders), grasped Raghu Tiadi's hands and begged: " You're a big man. You command respect in ten neighbouring villages. Surely you do not lack for anything that you too will look for a dowry to fill your house! Please accept my daughter as your wife and I'll remain eternally grateful to you. You will be doing a good turn, for which the gods will reward you. My daughter has strong stars in her horoscope and she will bring prosperity to whatever home she goes."

Raghu Tiadi was not easy to melt - he had heard enough spiels and sales pitch before—but a lingering look at the exquisite face of the girl touched a chord in his heart. On a sudden impulse he consented, and the wedding date was fixed on the spot. Sarami's eyes briefly met Sudam's. There was a flutter of gratitude in hers but all Sudam's piercing gaze held was the hint of an erotic welcome.

"Auntie," he gushed, only a few days after the wedding, "aren't you breathtakingly beautiful! The aunts before you were not equal to your toes! Uncle is one lucky man!" The new aunt had looked into the nephew's eyes: was he being facetious? A bitter question flashed through her mind: What about your new aunt's luck? Or are girls from poor families not supposed to have any? But her face remained as serene and her lips as tightly shut as ever. It was her first lesson in deceit in her husband's place and in the days ahead she would need it aplenty. She would have to learn to stifle her innate candour, honesty of opinion and easy manners. She was an aunt to Sudam and must continue as such, and as nothing else, in the young man's eyes. He could afford to behave like a lecher; society wouldn't condemn a man as much as a woman. One little scandal and Sarami would be handed a one-way ticket to purgatory; no amount of penance would absolve her of her crime.

Sudam married shortly afterwards and got a fat dowry. He kept it all but sent his wife back to her parents before the year was out. Obviously she wasn't as pretty as the dowry: she was toothy, squint-eyed, pitch-dark and loud-mouthed. "Display one girl and palm off another? They dare do this to me?" was what Sudam alleged. God alone knew the truth. Not long afterwards he married again. His second wife was not half as beautiful as Sarami, although in a matter of speaking, quite nicely put together, but that hardly mattered anyway, for a few days after the wedding she drowned in the family pond. No one knew whether it was an accident or a suicide. Evidently Sudam wasn't lucky in marriage. Nonetheless there was no dearth of girls, and the young man was still in his prime.

Meanwhile it warmed Raghu Tiadi's heart no end that his nephew had taken to his wife regardless of her aloofness and unmistakable display of annoyance. Of late she had badgered her husband one time too many: "Why don't you break with Sudam? Just because I'm around to work myself to death and keep the house, the fellow doesn't seem to bother whether his wives live or die, stay or leave. I can't be expected to look after him forever. In the future our own family will grow..."

Raghu Tiadi turned a deaf ear. Weren't women proverbial house-wreckers? Why start worrying before the family has expanded? Cross that bridge only when you come to it. Moreover Sudam wouldn't be without a wife for long. His horoscope indicated a bad patch for three years but after that everything would be all right. Split with a nephew? No way, a nephew was as good as a son. The trouble was that Sarami was not prepared to look upon Sudam as one. Petty, jealous, selfish women! Take Sudam. He never complained about his aunt. On the contrary, her name was on his lips all the time. Ten words from him would fetch a monosyllabic reply from her. Never once did she pull the sari off her head and show him her moon-face. Why be so stiff, so stand-offish? After all she was his aunt, wasn't she, although some seven or eight years younger? And wasn't an aunt the same thing as a mother? Besides Sudam was such a help. What would Raghu Tiadi do without him? He was freed from everyday cares and anxieties only because of this young man, who looked after the land and farming, the farmhands and harvests; he made it possible for the old man to devote his time to worship, adjudication meetings, teaching Sanskrit, and reciting scriptures. Raghunath Tripathy, alias Raghu Tiadi, was a learned person who had a name in society; people stepped back when he passed by. Wasn't Sarami a lucky woman to have become his wife? What did it matter whether she was the third or the fourth? She must thank the good karma of her previous births.

A woman's good fortune was judged by the social standing of her husband, the amount of jewellery she could laden herself with, the quality of food she ate, the weave of the clothes she wore—her state of her mind, happiness, emotional fulfilment, wishes all counted for nothing. Better that way, otherwise poor Sarami would have chosen to drown herself. She had learnt not to reflect, not to mull things over, and not to dwell on her condition; she had painfully acquired the habit of not thinking too much about herself. The abyss of darkness within her was fathomless and frightening. Sometimes she wondered what would happen to her if she lost her looks and turned into an ugly toad. Anything could happen. As long as she lived with her parents a fire had been in her stomach, but ever since she moved into her husband's home it had moved to her heart. The fire in the belly could be extinguished with food, but neither food nor clothes nor jewellery could douse the flames in her heart. On the contrary, the tongues leapt higher and higher. Sarami would gaze at herself, her beautiful body in an exquisite sari and bedecked with jewellery and her face would darken with anguish.

She had everything; yes she had everything she wanted. Raghu Tiadi never denied his wife the good things. To say that she was virtually like a queen was no exaggeration. Nobody ever surprised Raghu Tiadi being harsh to her. As the saying goes, he kept her on a pedestal. If despite all this she wasn't happy, she had no one but herself to blame. Admittedly Raghu Tiadi was a lot older and had lost his looks because of smallpox, but that didn't mean he was a lesser man. Why, he was in the pink of health, his manliness undiminished. Although he favoured his game leg, the ground literally shook when he walked. His emergence from his doorway—lines of shining sandal paste across the wide forehead beneath his bald dome—reminded many of Lord Jagannath's procession during his ceremonial chariot ride. He had successfully impregnated his young wife not once but twice, and in quick succession too; the blighted woman had only herself to blame for the miscarriages; they were no reflection on Raghu Tiadi's masculinity. Yes, yes, Sarami was squarely to blame. Particularly when there was no comfort under the sun that she lacked—she had plenty of food, clothes, jewellery! Perhaps all that had made her too lazy to even hold on to the foetus in her womb. Whereas her own poor mother, waging a daily battle against hunger and poverty, had ritually delivered babies every second year until she finally dried up, Sarami, on the other hand, had become too pampered in her husband's home. Even she herself sometimes tended to agree with this view. How she wished she had had two or three children! Then there would have been no free time to look into the depths of her soul. Everyday cares would have ensured that life passed faster and the hungry looks, the suggestive gestures, the audacious flirtations of her brother-in-law Dibakar and nephew-in-law Sudam wouldn't have troubled her so much.

To think one time she had nearly married Dibakar! The match had come unstuck at the last moment because her father could not scrape up the two thousand rupees Dibakar had demanded. The same fellow who had rejected her for the blessed money was now so full of love for her, the scoundrel!

But no matter how hard she steeled herself, how rudely she behaved towards Dibakar and Sudam, she couldn't hide from herself that she secretly relished the advances of the young wastrels. Sometimes when she served Sudam food, the fellow made a point of grasping her hands to say "Enough, enough, aunt!" and although she jerked her hands free and scolded him sternly "Why do you have to grab my hands? It's enough if you speak. I can still hear very well", she did feel giddy and delirious at the touch, her face aflame, her heart pounding away like a husking paddle. "My dear lovely aunt," Sudam would flirt outrageously, "I'm forced to hold your lovely hands because I'm afraid my words don't ever enter your beautiful ears!" Sarami would shriek, a flaming snake of desire slithering inside her entrails, "There's God above, Sudam. He's watching. You're going over the limits of decency. An aunt is like a mother." Sudam would burst into a guffaw: "You wouldn't have become my aunt if your poor father had been able to scrape up a good dowry. Don't think I didn't notice the look in your eyes the day Uncle and I turned up at your place to see you. Don't tell me you didn't feel attracted toward me, that you didn't find me desirable. Listen, ours is a quiet household and there's no one around to spy on us. It's an open secret that you don't get enough physical satisfaction from your husband."

Turning crimson as much from anger as from contempt, Sarami would rush into her bedroom, slam the door and throw herself on the bed, sobbing convulsively. A wild desire to spit Sudam in the face would seize her. When it was a question of marriage the fellow hadn't thought twice before rejecting her, but now he was so eager to start an affair! He might come to no harm but what would happen to her? Society would denounce her as an immoral bitch, a whore, a sinner. But who could she tell all this to? Once or twice she had tried to tell her husband ever so subtly, but the old man had retorted, fixing her with a hard, one-eyed stare, "Don't ever talk against our innocent Sudam. If he wanted to have you for himself he could've had got you on a platter. What was there was to prevent him from marrying you? Remember, I decided to step in only after he had turned you down. How can you insinuate these things against him?"

More than Sudam it was Raghu Tiadi who was responsible for her unenviable plight. He had damned her by his kindness. Surely her father could have found a young man for her, even if only from a nondescript family. She would no doubt have had a tougher life, maybe she would have had to work like a donkey, but anything was better than the kind of deprivation she was condemned to. Raghu Tiadi could give her the moon but not the physical bliss and pleasure for which she ached and ached no end. Their cohabitation was and would always remain an act of deceit, a sham, a pain. On the other hand, although with one part of her mind she hated Sudam and Dibakar, with another she feasted her eyes on their handsome, muscular physiques. A stray touch sent her pulse racing wildly, her heart beating furiously. Sometimes when Dibakar playfully tugged at the end of her sari she was scared she might swoon; she could hardly speak, she stuttered, stammered, and became tongue-tied. True, she was able to fend off their advances but could she dam the surging tides of desire and passion in her heart? When her marriage with Raghu Tiadi was being finalized, her parents should have realized that the man was old enough to be her father and could give her no physical satisfaction. But did they give it a thought? Raghu Tiadi too should have given it one. But did he? All of society should have protested against the mismatch. But did it? And now there were the likes of Dibakar and Sudam hovering around her to take full advantage of it. How they ogled her and propositioned her at every turn! Leave alone the most virtuous woman, if you work on a goddess ceaselessly, sooner or later she'll give in—it's as simple as that. In fact, the deeper the need the faster the opposition ended, sweeping aside the barricades of taboo society artfully clamped on relationships between a sister-in-law and a brother-in-law, an aunt and a nephew, and between cousins. Swept away like dry leaves in a torrent. Hunger made a person lose all sense of morality, drove him to beg crumbs from any source, and compelled him to left-overs on the sly. No matter what little saints, holy men, chaste people posed as, deep inside they were tormented souls on fire; hungry, tormented souls, driven by lust.

There were examples galore, many of them from that very village. Similar events might well have occurred elsewhere, in other villages as well. Nothing under the sun can remain forever under wraps. Yet the ones who ate the forbidden fruit nonchalantly wiped their lips and continued to pretend they were holier-than-thou, purer than the sacred waters of the Ganges, more sacrosanct than the consecrated prasad of the gods. Many clandestine affairs were embarked upon. Take the relationship between a man and his wife's sister, for example, or between a woman and her husband's brother, or between a woman and her god-brother. On the outside it was all very prim and proper, very correct, with just a whiff of flirtation maybe but nothing discordant, displeasing to the eyes, but inside it was all body. Something society was only too well aware of. At times the body drove one so crazy that he or she broke even bigger taboos. Perhaps, in the ultimate analysis, there was only one relationship which remained beyond the pale of corruption— the relation between a mother and her child. Everything else could prove rotten, even the relation between a father and a daughter, oh the shame of it! Man was nothing if not an animal underneath his clothes. Not long ago in this neighbourhood one wretched girl had chosen to hang herself because of the persistent attentions of her own father. There was a clandestine affair between a widowed aunt and her nephew which produced a child, whose dead body was discovered under the screw pine bushes at the edge of the village. In another incident, a man split open the skull of his brother because of the brother's carryings-on with his wife. For many a woman the loving attention of their devoted god-brothers had taken the sting out of their long separations from their husbands, who had to remain away from home on work. There were many, many more instances. But not a ripple on the surface— all was very placid, fine, within bounds.

Sarami was not the only one of her kind in the village— there were quite a few second and third wives, and none of them badly off either; in fact, they lived quite happily with their decrepit husbands, who were also dark and ugly into the bargain. How outrageously they flaunted their clothes, jewellery, authority and offspring! But were they really happy? Didn't they have regrets? How was it that not a shadow of their internal turmoil showed on their faces? How did they manage to look so serene, calm, collected? What were they made of—flesh and blood, or wood, stone and metal? Where had they put their minds—in a cave? And shut the mouth of the cave with a slab of stone? Did their bodies clamour for nothing besides food, clothes and jewellery? That was hard to accept. Why, Sarami was afraid that her mind and body were ready to betray her at the slightest provocation. How her mind yearned, hungered, lusted! Were there any tricks to wish one's mind away?

If only she could ask those women on the quiet, "Do you really find the social canons as sacred as the scriptures? Don't you ever feel tempted to break them? Don't you ever feel tormented? How do you manage to put on such serene expressions? If you are above all torment, what's the secret?" But she knew she could never bring herself to ask these questions. She could do so only at the risk of revealing herself, rendering herself vulnerable to tongue-wagging. The whole village would be abuzz with gossip: Sarami's got a filthy mind; all she ever thinks of is sex; she can't be too far from the path of adultery and infidelity. Without committing any wrong she would be roundly condemned as a whore, a sinner and an immoral woman, her reputation in tatters. Just as society sometimes dismissed the truth as idle gossip it could seize hold of a rumour and hammer it into a truth. Truth and rumour were like two sides of the same coin, and how quickly both travelled through the air! Better to keep her thoughts to herself. Thank God, thoughts were invisible. What total chaos there would have been otherwise! Would it ever have been possible to maintain even one perfect relationship, be it between a man and his wife or between a sister-in-law and a brother-in-law, or between cousins? All of society would be turned on its head. The flaming red vermilion dot on a woman's forehead was only a facade; she sinned enough in her mind to be damned to perdition until the end of eternity.

Sarami's self-flagellation often left her mind lacerated and badly bloodied. Her conscience was like a shark-tail whip — sharp, thorny, stinging. Ultimately that was what kept an affair away, though starting one or even several at the same time would have been terribly easy. A lonely house, the quiet afternoons; a deserted backyard, the dark evenings. She could get as many men as she wanted. A tiny nod from her and droves of brothers-in-law, nephews-in-law, uncles-in-law, stiff-lipped village elders, pontificating priests, stern-faced guardians of morals, men of high principles would have descended on her backyard, barnyard, pond-bank, cowshed, seeking trysts; and no one would have been the wiser. They could come and go each at his appointed hour, without bumping into one another. There wouldn't have been a blot on their reputation; not a blot on Raghu Tiadi's either. And of course Sarami's virtue would be left as dazzlingly bright as ever. Everything would continue smoothly, just as the hidden lives of all others did. But who prevented her? Who stopped her from crossing the strait of morality and fidelity? Sometimes she suspected that even her revered lord and master too was encouraging her to stray from the straight and narrow path. Why else did he leave a young and beautiful wife alone in the house under the care of a virile young nephew and stay away for days on end on the pretext of arbitrating disputes, giving scholarly advice and what not? Didn't a worldly-wise man like him know the consequences? Sudam might be his nephew, his blood relation, but he was nothing to Sarami. A little change in the script and the young hound could well have become her husband. A towering rage would possess her at times—a rage directed as much against herself as against her parents, her husband, society, the gods, everyone; her tortured soul sometimes taunted her to go whoring around to her heart's content. But a stern voice from within would stop her—what was it, her ego, her samskara, her notions of self-respect, her ideals of perfect womanhood? Adultery, she knew, was like a bowl of borrowed curry— good enough only for a gulp or two, it could never amount to a square meal. It would never fully sate her appetite, but leave her reputation in the mud. Even if it remained under wraps, she would never be able to hold her head high the rest of her life, forever ashamed to face herself.

But those who erred the most, those who made a profession of seducing and bedding women other than their wives, were the first to vilify an erring woman: "There goes the adulterous whore, pity her poor husband!" Sarami could never in her dreams bring herself to be reviled by these lowlifes. Even Sudam, who never ceased his broad hints, was scared of her. One frown from her petrified him into a block of wood. If she gave in to the temptations of her flesh even once, this very same Sudam would start treating her like a doormat. Once he was past the first flush of the fling he would seize every opportunity to rub her infidelity in. Life would become intolerable.

In fact, although her physical craving was as deep as an ocean her mental resolve was as hard as a mountain. One pitted against the other in a no-holds-barred fight; no quarter neither given nor expected. Sarami was a battle-scarred ground.

Just as the molten fire in the womb of the earth sometimes

flares—the fiercer the fire the greater the intensity of the tremor—and breaks free, spitting smoke, lava and ash, burying green vegetation, ruining nature, underlining its own ugliness, the repressed sexual desires smouldering within Sarami would sometimes erupt like a volcano. It was then that she went into sobbing hysterics, uncontrollably, unpredictably. Raghu Tiadi, with his slack, ageing muscles and slothful manhood, completely failed to rein her in and would steal away like a thief into the farthest corner of his verandah, subdued, crestfallen, morose, his copper-coloured face turning bitter black, ruing the day he had wedded a girl who was to bring him shame one day.

When Sarami was in the grip of hysteria, even the entire womenfolk of the neighbourhood could not curb her. It took five or six stout, strong-bodied hunks to pin her to the ground, their eager hands groping, probing, squeezing, caressing, and assuaging her body. After the spell passed, she would sit up, chastened, her face back behind her veil, biting her tongue in regret. Much as her blood boiled at the sight of the lusty young fellows crowding around her like vultures around a carcass, she had only herself to blame for making a spectacle of herself. What evil spirit had gotten into her and prodded her into such a shameless show!

In the beginning Raghu Tiadi and the relations thought that perhaps an evil spirit had temporarily possessed Sarami or a sorcerer had cast a spell on her. Some said it could be acute stomach-ache or some kind of extreme physical pain. But Sarami didn't respond to any cure—neither medicine nor exorcism. The doctors proved as helpless as the exorcists. In the end, people came to only one conclusion: "The girl is shamming! Can't you see how quickly her pain vanishes once four or six young men hold her down? What does that mean? She's dying for you-know-what, the bitch, the immoral bitch! Poor Raghu Tiadi, he brought shame on himself by marrying a third time. But a wife who isn't satisfied with her lawfully wedded husband, be he old, ugly or pockmarked, is a whore to the core."

Sarami couldn't prevent tongues from wagging. The only way out was to stop having hysterical fits, but that was something over which she had no control. The bouts came over her with embarrassing regularity, sometimes three or four times a month, in spite of having hardened her mind to stone. The stronger her resolve, the more determined her efforts to avert her eyes from men who made eyes at her, the more intense her afflictions. The very young men she kept at bay were the ones to feel, fondle, caress and squeeze her back to her senses. Could she ever tell them the truth? Why couldn't she keep her mind in check? Why was the mind so devious?

Time passed — weeks, months, years, decades; and Sarami's afflictions lessened and then suddenly disappeared altogether. She became normal. Her life became normal. In due course she became a mother, then a mother-in-law, and finally a grandmother. But the scandal of her youthful disgrace was not entirely forgotten or forgiven. Sometimes when there were quarrels, the relations and neighbours did not shy away from rubbing it in. Sarami couldn't answer back, for she indeed had had that horrible disease when she was newly married.

The other day when the young second wife of old Manu Rath was wallowing in the grip of hysteria, the whole village turned up to witness the drama. Four or five hefty young fellows were told to hold her down. That's what she needs, the immoral bitch, people openly commented. Poor Manu Rath's fair name was in the mud.

Sarami, old, bent, shrivelled, stood a little straighter, as if to get a kink out of her back, and looked around. She knew them — the ones who had their saris over their heads and easy judgements on their eager lips. She knew them all inside out, the depth and extent of their chastity and fidelity, or rather the lack of it. Gathered here to castigate Manu Rath's wife, eh? That was a crime in Sarami's eyes. If it was a crime on the part of a young woman not to be satisfied with her old, decrepit husband, it was a bigger crime to expose her sad failing in public.

"Listen you all!" She faced the crowd, her brittle voice catching from rage. "The young woman here is suffering from an abominable affliction. Pity her by all means, but give her the respect she deserves. Praise her for her conviction, for she didn't give up the principles of chastity and fidelity and rush to seek solace in clandestine affairs. That's why the fire within her drives her plumb crazy sometimes. There are many women present who took the easy way out to douse their fires, but not this poor girl. She did not want to open her doors to other men and keep pretending she was virtuous. You dare denounce her just because she didn't? Come on, ladies, come, come my pretties, my beauties, come and swear on the heads of your husbands and sons that not a single dirty thought ever flitted across your minds!"

She paused and added, "Society is cruel to women. Like cattle, girls are given away to old men against their wishes. They have no say in the selection of their mates. Why? Don't women have minds? Are they all body and no mind? Have they been made only to eat, work and bear children? Yes, the body can be satisfied, but not the mind. And a dissatisfied mind can never extinguish the fire raging within. So in the end it's society which compels a woman to acts of immorality. A few who decide not to fall from their convictions convulse occasionally like this girl here. All you virtuous whores—have you no pity that you dare assemble here to castigate this poor little thing? Why are you so eager, so enthusiastic to witness her shameful plight? Get going. Go away. Leave before I give out all your dirty little secrets. Do you think old Sarami doesn't know what each of you has been up to?"

The women were hushed. The contempt in Sarami's old withered face was as dark and dense as their hidden sins.

The poor young wife of Manu Rath lay like a wick burnt from end to end—alone, away from the crowd, aloof as it were from society itself. Sarami hobbled over to her and sat down by her side. With her dry, decrepit, wrinkled hands she gently wiped the stains of the stigma from the forehead of the young woman. But could she be rid of the stigma for a sin she had never committed in the first place?

Hunger

Translated by **Adyasha Das**

Maina's face glowed with pleasure as she heaped rice and curry on Mahani's plate. The happiest moments of Maina's life were when she sat near Mahani, served him and fed him lovingly. As Mahani relished the delicious rice and curry, he would chide her, "Have you kept something for yourself? I know you too well. You must have surely put everything on my plate. How can you women starve religiously, for us?"

Maina would blush with a queer, proud pleasure, as though Mahani's words were the ultimate tribute to her womanhood. "If the husband eats well," she would reply, "the wife has her fill. Your leftover is the sacred gift of God for me; even a little of that is enough to satiate me."

Mahani would drink the small pot of water, kept especially for him. Letting out a great belch of contentment, he would try to flatter Maina, "But it is not true of all women. My friend Bisia's wife has the greater share and serves almost nothing to

Bisia!" Maina would shudder in disgust, "Ugh! Greedy woman! How hateful! Of what use is her life?"

Mahani would continue to wax eloquent, "Forget her. She is an illiterate bum." Maina would ask, "But what about our mistress? Does she content herself with the leftovers of master? Does she serve him the choicest dishes?" Mahani would laugh, "Do you know, they eat at the same table, in the true sahib style. The cook serves them equally, not more to master and less to our mistress. I always feel as though it is a hotel, not a home, that they are college-going friends, not a married couple. Our mistress's lifestyle never fails to amaze me!"

Main's eyes would widen in horror, "My God! Is it true? God, how can a wife bring herself to eat along with her husband? How can she even swallow the food? So what if they are wealthy? She should be ashamed of herself."

Maina did not think it possible for any woman to eat more, at the cost of her half-fed husband and children. If the impossible would ever occur, the sun would rise in the west. All mankind would be cursed to an animal birth. Even a bird feeds her little ones first. Mahani had once recounted the horrors of the great famine, when mothers would snatch food from their children; even devour their flesh to stay alive. Maina would break into a cold sweat, as she listened to Mahani's frightening tales. The very roots of her hair would tingle. The horrifying picture of a mother gnawing into her child's flesh would flash before her eyes. Maina's head would go into a dizzy spin, her tears blinding her and blurring Mahani's face. She would hide her face in Mahani's lap, like taking refuge in her mother's lap, when scared of the dark. Through her sobs, she would mumble, "Oh God! It is better to die. Even among animals there is no such brutal murder of children." Mahani would gently comfort her, "The famine happened so long ago! It is more a story now than the reality; you are crying as though you saw it yesterday! How can you manage the tough job of running a household, with such a tender heart? Which family has ever been spared its share of misery and misfortune? Mother of two, aren't you? And how will you bring them up, with such a soft heart?"

As if reliving the past, an entranced Maina would say, "It may be a tale now, but it did happen once! The mother of this land had become a devil. May God never curse humanity with a similar situation, ever again? May all mothers keep their children alive, even if it means giving their blood?"

Mahani would laugh at her words and say, "The famine can no longer touch our country. Times have changed. You have made a mountain out of a molehill; you are crying for no good reason." And with that, Mahani would go to attend to his work.

Nevertheless, Maina would brood. It is a popular belief that poverty debases. Which family enjoys the happiness and contentment of the harvesting season constantly? Maina's small family of four, too, had to face its share of rainy days. Of course, everyone had a liberal share of rice, but curry, rice-cakes and other delicacies were strictly rationed. Mahani was right. The great famine had never again succeeded in spreading its tentacles in the country. But inflation was a disease that had come to stay, what with prices shooting sky-high. And it had been spreading like an incurable patch of leprosy. Despite her poverty, Maina's nature had remained unchanged. The curry that she prepared was lovingly served to her husband and children. For her, rice, with salt and green chili was good enough. Was it not ridiculous that women could not ever manage without curry or a side dish? Sometimes she did enjoy a little leftover curry. But she had never seen her mother having a proper meal in her lifetime. The children would always clamour for a mouthful from their mother's plate, even when their bellies were full. No matter how meagre the meal, mother would always share her food. Maina was her mother's worthy daughter.

If ever rice-cakes were prepared, she would put a tiny piece in her mouth, to taste. After her husband and kids had had their fill, she sometimes felt like having a few, if there were any left behind. But she could never bring herself to eat them. The children rarely had a chance to relish their favourite rice-cakes; they would surely want to have them later in the day too. She felt no rancor at the sacrifice. On the contrary, a strange contentment would envelope her. And when the children would lick their lips, utterly delighted at the second helping of cakes, Maina's bliss would know no bounds. She would feel the sweet taste of cake in her mouth. Mahani would say, "A woman like you must be one in a billion." Maina would laugh off the compliment and say, "The heart of every mother feels the same way. When I see the smiling faces of my children, my hunger dies." Through good and bad times, Maina managed her home. Poverty was never considered an unavoidable obstacle. But one day, the moon disappeared and Maina's family was plunged into the depths of darkness. Mahani lost his job. For no good reason, he was retrenched. How was the family to survive? Mahani went to work on daily wages. Somehow, life went on. Maina skipped her meals to feed her kids, with the meagre sum Mahani brought home. Then, suddenly Mahani was afflicted with a strange disease and was confined to bed. There was no money for food, leave aside his treatment.

Maina took up work as a maidservant at the master's house, washing dirty dishes in the mornings and evenings, clothes too, sweeping and cleaning the house twice a day for a paltry sum of thirty rupees. That meant a rupee a day for a family of four. Mahani's treatment, the kids' occasional illness, food and clothing, everything had to be managed in that sum. Yet Maina was not disheartened. She gathered all her courage for the sake of her family. She had only one meal in a day. And to add to her miseries, the work was back-breaking. She knew she should get another job to supplement her income. But she felt drained of all strength. Would she be able to manage two jobs? And if she fell ill, what would become of her family?

Maina was getting weaker by the day. Hunger, like ash-covered ember, was smouldering deep within her. There was no saying when it would erupt. If she jumped into the well and took her life, to escape the inescapable iron grip of hunger, what would happen to her family? Maina could no longer work properly. The mistress had been threatening to fire her, if she didn't improve. Now she had started deducting her wages for her occasional absence. But how could Maina help it? She dragged herself around, trying to do her best.

This month, her salary was fifteen rupees less. She had borrowed that amount for Mahani's medicines. How could she meet the various expenses for a month with the rest of her salary? The hearth had not been lit for days together in her house. Everyone tried to kill their hunger with the titbits she bought. The children could no longer put up a fight, though, God knows, they might start begging any day, so unbearable was the need for food. Mahani's incurable disease was slowly driving him mad. He demanded food day and night and was not concerned about anyone else.

The continuous hard work and hunger took its toll on Maina. She came down with fever. After eight endless days and nights, she dragged herself to her mistress's house, to get few morsels of food. The fever had covered her face with boils. The world looked pitch-dark, so blinded was she with hunger. There wasn't a grain of rice in the house, no food, no money. While she was bedridden, Mahani had blown her salary on sweetmeats.

The world crashed around Maina when she saw another maidservant bustling around in the mistress's house. A disheartened Maina retraced her steps. There was no hope for her now. Sick as she was, who would give her a job in her present condition? Till she regained her health to get a new job, she decided to beg. Why should she be ashamed? Wasn't the entire family dependent on her?

Maina combed the streets, begging, but in vain. Has anyone ever satisfied one's hunger by begging? Maina had not cooked for the last eight days. But an angry, hungry fire was rearing in everyone in her family. The alms she got were insufficient, even for the children. Poor, diseased Mahani was worse than a child, with his demands for food. Forced to starve most of the time, the children were like emaciated skeletons. They had been robbed of the strength to even speak. Only their blank stare followed Maina. Mahani thrashed about in frustration, as hunger tore at his insides.

Maina had not seen a handful of rice for some days now. She filled her belly with tap water instead. Her day's begging yielded almost nothing. She had a sickening intuition that she would collapse one of these days. How long could she hold out against this all-consuming hunger? The rest of the family would follow her to the other world. At least, she would not be there to bear the loss of others.

That day, Maina got a few handfuls of rice from a kind lady, the fungus-covered rice of some forgotten time. Yet she was filled with gratitude; the lady could easily have fed the rice to her cow than give it away!

As she tied the rice to the end of her sari, Maina was filled with renewed vigour; at last, her children would get to eat some steaming hot rice today. Even Mahani would have a handful; she would drink the thick, syrupy water that was left behind. Of course she would share it with Mahani, for it gave strength. At last her children would live.

Someone within her screamed, "Maina! Do you want to die?" She boldly replied, "Yes! I will die for my children and my husband and go to heaven. I will be eternal."

Maina put the rice on to boil and went to her children. She looked at Mahani. All of them seemed lifeless. Mahani asked in a weak whisper, "Did you get anything?" Hope flickered in the dull eyes of the children. Maina stammered, "Each of you will get some hot rice today. The rice is already cooking." The children chirped faintly, "Cook it fast, please. A bit longer and we will die of hunger." "Give me more," demanded one voice. Immediately, a second voice rose in protest, "No, I'll have more. I'm ravenous!". Then Mahani's voice, "Please give me a good share. God bless you."

Maina could shed no tears. The searing heat of hunger had dried up her well of tears. She ran back to the confines of the kitchen. She slumped down there, with her legs stretched out. As she fed another piece of wood to fire, the hunger in her stomach burst into a volcano of flames. Maina ignored it. Why should she be afraid of this fire, when she had vowed to starve herself to death for the sake of her children?

The higher the flames rose from the stove, the greater was the hunger in everyone. The rice and hunger steamed in unison. The intoxicating aroma of the fungus-filled rice increased their hunger a hundredfold. All soaked in the heavenly smell, their eyes, nose and ears alert. Six burning eyes were riveted on Maina, all pleading, "Give me more!"

Maina was flustered. Her hands trembled as she brought down the vessel from the stove. She started serving steaming rice in three battered aluminium plates. She was undecided about who to give more. She would be unfair to Mahani, if the distribution was equal. But her pleading children unsettled her mind. With her back to her waiting family, Maina kept trying with a handful of rice, shifting it, in turns, among the plates. But however much she tried, the distribution didn't seem right. Like the small end of her sari, if she covered one portion more, the other remained bare. In the background, three voices were screaming in unison, asking for more. Strangely, the desperate voices of her dear ones seemed to her like the furious yelping of hungry dogs. The fire roared in the empty stove. Maina didn't have the strength to throw water and put it out.

Maina, too, had a fire raging in her. There was no way of getting rid of it. She did not have a share of the rice. With great difficulty, she finished serving. Morsels of hot rice clung to her fingers. She had an urge to lick her hands clean. She rolled her tongue over her fingers. Aaahh! Whoever said rice was not tasty? It was tastier than nectar. She continued sucking her fingers, like a hungry child. Her children were shrieking like kittens, "What are you doing, mother? Are you eating the rice? Oh please! We can't get up and go to you. We just don't have the strength. We feel as though we are dying. Dear mother! Why don't you reply?"

After calling out to her lovingly several times, Mahani was gnashing his teeth in rage, "Bitch! What are you up to, sitting there? Can't you reply? Get the rice, all of it, damn you. I will have the whole of it. Don't you dare give it to anyone else. I am warning you. Let them die. I'll drink your blood if you so much as offer it to them." And the children's unending refrain, "Let father die. Give us the rice. Hurry!"

Maina was deaf to all. Like a calf tugging at the dried up udders of its mother after milking, she continued to suck her fingers, one after the other. She dipped her fingers into the heaped plates. And sucked them rapturously. Ahh! What a divine taste! What a maddening smell!

Suddenly, the demon in Maina's belly broke the fetters and leapt out. The cruel, horrifying, blind, omnivorous demon snatched handfuls of rice from all the plates and gobbled them down. Like a brood of chick under attack, having lost their siblings to a fearful hawk, the terrified children screeched. Mahani clawed the earth in blind rage.

Maina was thrashing the demon with all her might, with the red-hot iron rod she used to poke at the embers, "Get away! Go! My children are starving! My husband too. Don't snatch food away from their mouth. Better to burn to death in this fire. Die! Die!"

But the demon did not heed her anguished cries. With her back to the children, she was using both her hands to gulp down mouthfuls of hot, steaming rice. The plates were now empty—all of them, licked clean by the demon. Maina felt faint. After cleaning off the last morsel, the demon had crept back to the dark cavern of Maina's stomach. The whole world was quiet. Almost.

Maina belched in contentment. God knows after how many days she had got to eat some rice. The angry roar of hunger in her had died down. If she had some water on top of this, it would see her through for some days.

But Maina shuddered in horror to see her hands were covered with lumps of blood. She had not eaten rice. She had drunk handfuls of blood, human blood, pouring from the torn hearts of her children, her husband. She rubbed her eyes and looked again. There was blood everywhere, on the plates, on her hands. No sound came from behind her. She could not bring herself to turn round and look. She licked her lips and tasted the warm, sticky, salty blood. From where was all this blood pouring onto her lips? She touched her face. Blood coursed down her eyes, onto her lips; the blood of her husband, of her own children. Maina rolled over, laughing hysterically, as though she had lost her mind.

She was talking to herself, "Mahani and his tall talk that

great famines do not return. Men aren't forced to eat human flesh to survive. But a mother tore apart the heart of her children and drank their blood! She became a demon, even without a famine."

Such a mother didn't deserve to live. Maina was banging her head on the floor, still with her back to her family. The blood she had drunk only moments ago, was now pouring from her forehead. If only she could feed that blood to her children! Even that wasn't possible. The world was hungry. On all sides omnivorous hunger stalked about, with wide open jaws. The eager earth was sucking up the blood dripping from Maina's forehead, like a cruel demon - Mother Earth!

■

Ketaki Grove

Translated by **Aparna Satpathy**

The realization that I too had aged hit me for the first time when I met Subha. Though I was due to retire from my government job in a year, the fact that I had grown old had never before been brought home so emphatically to me.

Subha was much younger than I and such a baby-face that I'd never imagined she would look old one day. I was meeting her after thirty two years. I was saddened to see that not only did she look old, she actually was old. As for me, I could no longer deny the truth of my own advancing years.

Of course, even if one were to acknowledge the passing of the years, where is the time to dwell in it? Who allows you the luxury of reveling in it? Your wife, children, grandchildren, whom will you plead with to leave you alone because you've grown old? Who among them enjoys perennial youth that makes it all right for you to bow out of an active existence, pleading old age? Actually, the older you get the more mired you are in all kinds of worldly affairs and illusions. One is not a yogi. The

Government declares you old at the age of fifty eight but you cling on, like a politician clings to his seat unto the last. Besides, as a member of the middle class, when are your dreams ever fulfilled, and when are you ever absolved of all responsibilities – your life partner is not your wife but your never-ending need. Some people in my position believe that it's foolish to chase dreams of becoming a millionaire, but we do, don't we, nevertheless?

Of course, I knew long before I raised a family that I was not destined to be rich. My family was in dire poverty when I cleared my matriculation. To continue with my studies I had to tutor students in my mama's village. My father, my uncle and I have always held that had I not wasted my study time giving tuitions, I would definitely have secured a first division. At the time, however, I was content to pass the intermediate and then my Bachelor of Arts.

Many boys from lower middle class families of my generation paid for their own education by giving tuition and, years later, engaged five private tutors each for their own offspring! I decided not to do this for my children even if I was financially in a position to do so, as a matter of principle; for if I did, my children, like Subha, would always depend for every small thing on their tutors.

Subha was so spoon-fed that not only was it necessary for me, her tutor, to do her math and drawing, but I also had to ghost-write the "Autobiography of a Cow" for her. Mercifully, since she was a student of class nine, Subha didn't have to write the cursive regularly. Otherwise, I would have had to do even that! I had no great expectations of Subha. I knew that passing the matriculation exam was a hobby for the delicate, pampered daughters of the rich and ranked alongside drawing designs with rice paste, embroidering "Sweet Dreams" on pillow covers (though bereft of any knowledge of the English language) and enshrining the good character certificate of God in the form of a "God is Good" picture and hanging it on the wall. All these achievements were then reeled off to impress prospective suitors and their nosy entourages.

I knew for sure that Subha would get married before she

passed matriculation because she was already twenty, having flunked twice in each class. I was also the oldest in my class as I had started my education late and then wasted more time in tutorial assignments. However, I must confess, I didn't want Subha to be married off immediately. There was no noble motive for this, merely an ambitious boy's selfish wish – I was paid handsomely by Subha's father and fed an occasional delicious meal, so I prayed to God to delay Subha's marriage by three, four years, just long enough for me to complete my BA. But why would any eligible bachelor postpone his nuptials in deference to my wishes?

Subha suddenly discarded the load of matriculation anxiety and instead donned the crown of marriage. After one last sumptuous feast, on the occasion of Subha's marriage, I began looking for another job. I never saw her bridegroom, who was a big officer, because he arrived, as all bridegrooms do, in the middle of the night. The desire to see Subha's bridegroom was not nearly strong enough to keep me awake.

I didn't stop dreaming my big dreams because of Subha. Nothing stops for anyone. After struggling for many years, I not only managed to pass my BA but my MA as well. Then I got married and settled down. There was neither the opportunity nor the need to keep track of Subha. I was completely caught up in my own life, the love of my wife, the drudgery of household affairs, disappointments on the job front, petty injustices, transfers from one place to another, new friends, the struggle to make ends meet, and survival in this competitive world; and now I stood on the brink of retirement.

Some years ago, Subha's son had scored a distinction and his name was printed in the newspaper. The newspaper mentioned that he was the son of Shri Manmohan Mohanty and Shrimati Sobharani Mohanty and the grandson of Chaudhary Jagmohan Ray. Of course, I immediately knew that Sobharani was Subha. There may not be much difference between these two names Subha and Sobha, but for me, the difference was significant. Why do people name their daughters after renowned beauties – Sobha, Sundari, Menaka, Urvashi – each followed by a Rani? For one thing, such names make them unnecessarily proud, especially if they are, in fact, endowed with some physical charm. But if the names are beautiful and they are not, then it gives them a sort of inferiority complex. Moreover, how many of them are lucky to be a rani, a queen? And even if they are, are they really happy? That was the reason why I had changed Sobha's name to Subha. But I was the only one who called her that. Anyway, if Subha had again become Sobha in her husband's home, what did I care? I had heard that her husband earned a lot, had power, fame and lot of property. He earned lakhs of rupees. He had given Subha her own car and driver.

I had to struggle to remember whether Subha was pretty, which only means that hers was not the extraordinary kind of beauty that gets indelibly impressed on one's mind, though, like every other girl of her age, Subha was endowed with a fresh innocence and a sweet, virginal charm that was pleasing to the eye. Some young rivers swell and overflow their banks, some are placid and steady. Subha was always grave and decorous even in the impulsive and unpredictable years of her youth and showed a wonderful sense of proportion in the amount she laughed and spoke. She did not do this deliberately. She was naturally grave. It is also entirely possible she was this way because of the scolding she received from me for not doing her homework regularly, and for her inability to grasp a point even after repeated explanations. Another reason could be that she was distracted most of the time- which is something quite natural at her age. Whatever the reason, the fact was that Subha was a quiet person.

On the day before she was to be married she came up to me. "Sir, I am very sad," she said, hesitantly.

"Why feel sad? Every girl has to get married one day."

"Yes but..."

"So, is it because you have to discontinue your studies?"

"No Sir, I am not at all sad about dropping out of school. I am not particularly fond of studies, you know that! It is good Baba allowed me to get married before the exam. Actually, I .... I am upset because there will be no more tuitions."

"Very strange! You need my tuition only because of your studies. You are not upset about having to discontinue your studies, but you are sad that the tuition would stop?" I burst out laughing.

"Sir, I am afraid that your graduation studies might stop. Everything happens as willed by God. If you are destined to pass, you will but…" I gave her a quizzical look as Subha blushed. As I stepped out into the rains lashing the city, her last words were still ringing in my ears. "Sir, you must come to my house."

It is my opinion that for girls "my house" is more important than "my husband." Woman just love being in charge of a house. They may not like the husband chosen for them but get along with their lives, concentrating all their attention on "my home." They may not be free to choose their husbands but when it comes to setting up a home, they are in full control. It is possible to get on with one's life without loving the husband, but it is well-nigh impossible to do so without loving one's home. Who knows if Subha's husband was to her liking or not? However, when she saw her new house, it must have met with her approval. A home must have blossomed with Subha at the helm, anointing everything with her auspicious touch, a home that was bound to fall apart without her.

After thirty two years I chanced on Subha in a saree shop. Grey hair, flab, black and red, betel-stained teeth with one gold-capped molar, heavy gold ornaments that dug into thick arms and neck, a round, plump face and dark patches under the eyes. I didn't recognize her but my eyes kept going back to her face. The abandon with which she was selecting sarees from a heap of very expensive ones indicated that she was a rich woman. It also indicated that she gave more important to her possessions and status than to herself. Even the salesman paid her more attention than he did me, probably a regular customer. I was trying he haggle down the price of a saree with a much more modest price tag, for my wife. The saree was beautiful. It caught the woman's eye. Then she looked from the saree to me. Suddenly, she got up and folded her hands, overwhelmed with joy.

"Sir, how come you are here, Sir?"

Taken aback I asked her who she was.

She replied, "Don't you recognize me? I am Subha." Her voice had cracked along with her face-she sounded as if her throat was choked with phlegm.

"No. Really, I could not. You have changed so much…"

"Sir, why don't you just say that I have grown old? I have three grandchildren. We are celebrating the youngest one's birthday-that is the reason I'm shopping. He is happy with anything. As for my daughter-in-law, she… "Subha gushed like a river overflowing its banks.

I said, "I read of your son's success in the newspaper. It is fortunate that he has turned out to be such an outstanding student."

"Exactly like his father. You know how intelligent I am."

Subha's voice was full of pride for her husband and son. I noted the totality of her happiness. Only mindless girls like Subha are capable of such happiness- if their children study well and their husbands earn good money, there can be no sorrow.

Subha whispered, "Sir, were you able to pass your graduation?"

I was momentarily taken aback. Nevertheless, the guileless question made it clear that even though Subha's appearance had changed, she had not. She remained as clueless as ever. It was obvious that she had no idea what I did or who I was. How does one answer such a question in a shop?

Ignoring the question, I said. "I was transferred to this place a year ago and will retire in a year's time. I am glad to have met one of my students after all this time". I asked her to give me her address. "I'll drop in some day," I said.

Subha took her husband's visiting card out from her purse and I cut the conversation short by taking it and leaving the shop abruptly. If she had asked me any more idiotic question- whether I ate good food, for instance- I would have completely lost my cool.

One day I decided to honour her request and look her up. At

least, she should know that though she had escaped her education by marrying early, I had not only passed my graduation, but my post-graduation too and had managed to get a prestigious job. I could afford fish, meat, milk, fruits and ghee. I did not have to depend on tuitions anymore. Her husband may be well to do, but I was not poor either, though one must admit it is not easy to run a middle class household in a country like ours.

When I reached Subha's house at five in the evening, she was sitting near a bucket full of milk. Seeing me she said, "You must have to buy milk. You could have got pure, unadulterated milk from us if you lived a little closer. We milk cattle throughout the year. I have become a veritable vendor, what with figuring out what to do with all this milk. "Nowadays, business on the domestic front like selling sarees, training dogs and selling milk has become the latest status symbol of the rich.

Subha hurriedly made some cheese and served me a full plate of nuts and sweets with great enthusiasm. Thirty two years ago, I would wolf down everything that she served and more often than not I did not have to eat supper afterwards. However, now when I saw so many delicacies in front of me, at that hour, I said, "So much? Am I a cow or a demon like Kumbhakarna? Besides, I have food restrictions. No sweets and nuts. I just want half of this piece of cheese."

Subha was aghast. She could not believe that I had acquired a rich man's blood.

"I am not lying. I ate a lot when I was young. Now my health does not permit any over-indulgence. A middle class man usually spends everything on food. Food is his chief luxury because he cannot afford any other." I wanted Subha to know that I maintained a reasonable middle class home.

"My doctor has also imposed severe food restrictions on me," said Subha, as she started devouring the sweets and nuts she had put out for me. "But who cares? Humans will die in any case, with or without food. Then why not die eating everything? I have never had any hobby other than eating."

Soon I became a regular visitor to Subha's house. Though

there was no real reason to go there, I felt I was neglecting my duty if I did not turn up every two or three days. My wife and children also met her once or twice and were treated very well. Subha too visited our place with her grandchildren. Her husband of course didn't have the time to come over, being a highly placed officer with many responsibilities – he even brought work home from the office, as if there was nothing more important than it. The life of officers like him is pathetic. It is as if they have nothing to live for, in spite of all the happiness in their personal and family lives. I have not misunderstood Subha's husband. I would have felt awkward if he had come to my house thinking that I was a middle-class man. I was not on friendly terms with him nor did I wish to be. The little I knew of him convinced me that he was quite the average husband, off-loading all the responsibilities of the household on his wife's shoulders, and residing in his own world.

People thought I was an old tutor hired for her three grand-children. Everyone called me "Sir." Sometimes I felt not just Subha's husband, grandchildren and servants, even her cattle probably called me "Sir" in their language.

What kept taking me back to Subha's place? Definitely not Subha, and there was no question of it being her pompous and prestige hungry husband. Nor was it the tasty food as I had made it a point not to partake of anything at her place, except tea. They made the most exquisite green-leaf tea. They normally made dust-leaf tea for visitors but I was treated to the regular family tea. What flavor! Milk, sugar - everything in the right proportion. Not once was the tea marred by an excess of milk or sugar, which is quite common in middle class homes like mine. Probably it was the cup of tea that drew me on my way back from office, like a sucking calf to its mother. Sometimes I used to ask for an extra cup. Subha's grandchildren had taken to calling me "Tea Sir."

Perhaps even the tea was not the main attraction. Perhaps it was her grandchildren; because mine did not stay with me, my affection for hers grew day by day. My trips to her house were so regular that if I missed going there one day, Subha would question me about it on my next visit. "Why didn't you come yesterday? The kids missed you so much. They made my life miserable. I waited until eight o'clock for my evening tea. Was there a problem?"

Very strange! How can she push and force me like that? Have I been bought by a cup of tea? As if I was a tutor at her place, and was bound to go there every day. I went there of my own volition. Who was she to question me? Without answering her question, I would say, "Today I have planned to have two or three cups of tea, so hurry up and bring them on. Now where are the kids?" and my anger would be diffused by the delicate aroma of the green-leaf tea wafting out of my cup.

Slowly I discovered that the quiet girl had become a garrulous woman. The past was prominent in Subha's conversation, while the present barely warranted a mention. She pined for her village, its river, mango groves, orchards and the forest of ketaki flowers. She missed her circle of friends. The conversation would invariably start with food and quickly move on how, although mangoes, guavas, plantains and berries were available in the city, some typical country fruits like gooseberries, blackberries and the like were not to be seen; how among a variety of nurseries and gardens, country flowers such as the blue lotus and the ketaki were conspicuous by their absence. How the sky here was lost among the skyscrapers, and the moon forever unnoticed in the light of the electric lamps, the sweet chirping of the birds in the madding din of the city, the sweet smell of the earth in the smoke and dust. How human nature was blunted by selfishness, and how distanced people were even from close friends! The walls of buildings touched each other but the people didn't. There was neither dawn nor dusk, nor time for anything.

"Sir, it is our great good fortune that you were able to find the time to look us up, though you didn't have to," Subha said one day. "Your presence makes me feel as it our ketaki grove has not yet died, the blue lotuses still bloom in our village pond, the smoke of each hut continues to curl upwards and merge with that coming out of others huts. People still send dishes prepared for dinner to each other's houses, and everybody has time for everyone else. I have not been to the village for a long time. After all, who is there now? Every relative of ours is settled in some town or the other. Our village has grown old; only poverty, disease, and old, unwanted people inhabit it. Sir, do you visit the village sometimes?"

I remembered how often I used to bring her the ketaki flower so her grandmother could make a catechu for her hair. I was adept at plucking the ketaki, at removing the dusky-green outer leaves with their long, needle-sharp edges, to reach the pale gold inner leaves and the flower inside, the color of old, rich silk. What fragrance! Subha liked to weave the leaves into her plait. Once she had told me, "The ketaki smells better than the catechu made from it. Grandmother unnecessarily destroys it to make the catechu."

What regret could Subha have amidst such plenty and fulfillment? Surely the limited vision of a simple-minded woman like Subha will not notice anything lacking, will it? How was it possible then that a germ of discontent lay hidden all these years, within this obese woman's body and thought? But slowly, observing Subha daily I was amazed that she was capable of fine thought; though if an outsider observed her, he would have thought her a complete bumpkin.

I have stopped going to Subha's place. I have decided not to. It is better not to face her again. I sometimes remember the loud voices of her grandchildren- "Tea Sir has come!", and the flavor of the tea. There is no fragrance in the tea at my place and no voices of grandchildren, either. Sometimes my feet turn on their own to Subha's house, but my judgment and conscience stop them from moving ahead.

The other day, a day of torrential rain, an unforgettable incident occurred as I sat relishing a cup of tea at Subha's, and I don't think it proper to go to her place now. Of course it happened so suddenly that even I was surprised. No one will know about it. Subha's husband, her well-established son, daughter, son-in-law, and daughter-in-law will never have a clue. Such a thing will never happen again. But then, what else is left to happen? The incident was conclusive. If I resume my tea-sessions now, sipping tea like a gentleman, or like the tutor of yesteryears, will it not be a farce? I won't ever have to meet Subha's husband-our earlier meetings were brief and superficial anyway-but I will have to face Subha. Maybe her eyesight is not as good as it once was but her vision certainly is. Will I be able to face her as I did before the incident, and what about Subha's feelings?

Oh God! Why did such an incident have to happen at this time now when we are both so old? Will our lives change because of it? Had the incident not taken place, would our lives be incomplete? Perhaps, had the incident never happened, we would not have experienced the self-truth we both discovered about ourselves. But is it proper for such a situation to arise at this age? Could it not have been averted? Of course she started it but is it possible for a thick headed, easily satisfied, middle-aged woman like Subha, to create such an improbable situation without any encouragement? I know now. Subha's fat body conceals feelings as refined as the sweetest music.

The human mind is like a ketaki grove. It is very difficult to reach it, but does the silent fragrance of the ketaki flower remain undiscovered? Is there ever a need for the Ketaki to shout and advertise itself? "I have beautiful fragrance. Come and smell me?"

After the incident, I realized that no girl is satisfied with a little bit, no girl is thick headed, and no girl ages. In one moment, Subha destroyed my strong male prejudice. Not only that, she also shook my unswerving opinion of myself. She has proved that neither of us has grown old. Old age is merely a shell- remove the shell, and within it brims the flavor of joy.

I do not blame Subha for the incident. My only regret is that what should have taken place thirty two years ago happened now. Who could benefit from the incident? The only outcome was that my visits to Subha's place came to an abrupt halt. Of course, Subha has not told me to stop coming, but I know that is the very least she expects of me. I know that even if I go back there, things will never be the same again. Perhaps the heart-wrenching rain was responsible for whatever happened that evening.

Nobody was at home. Her grandchildren had gone to their mama's place. The big house seemed as deserted and empty as a school building during the summer vacations. Just then it began to rain incessantly, as it had thirty two years ago.

Did the rain give a damn for the crops sure to be destroyed by the overflowing rivers? Did it stop for the houses that were being swept away by the floods? Once, on a similar day of rain, the twenty year old Subha had casually announced she was about to be married. She declared her sadness about her tuitions coming to an end. She invited me to visit her new home. She had looked different than any other bride-to-be. The innocent young thing was full of sympathy for the poor, young tutor whose tuition would stop, who would no longer get his tea and snacks, and whose dream to pursue higher education would remain unrealized.

Then, many years later, once again a day when it rained non-stop. Subha served me sizzling cheese balls, to counter the weather, she said, which I categorically refused. I saw the pained alas-this-man-is-not-fated-even-to-eat-fresh-food look writ large on Subha's face and thought," My God, so much anguish? Wasn't she overdoing the hurt?" Then I thought I saw Subha's eyes turn moist- maybe just drops of rain. Subha returned with a sugarless cup of tea for me. Her forehead and face were covered with beads of sweat.

And then a bolt of lightning struck. An oversized plantain tree that had been loaded down with a large bunch of plantain, collapsed. Oh Subha! Why did you do this? Have you taken me for a foolish, greedy and awkward man? Not everything is expressed verbally. Not everything is articulated in one lifetime. Don't you know that unsaid thoughts are deeper? The words one gropes for, struggling to convey a sentiment, can never match the eloquence and depth of feelings of the unsaid. Why don't you understand this, Subha? Who should know it better than you who have repressed so much tumult in her heart?

Oh why did you, in one second, Subha, make vulgar the secret words inscribed on the ketaki petals? Handing me the sugarless cup of tea, why did you abruptly say, "Sir, why didn't you speak your mind that night? Being a girl, how could I have been so bold myself?"

I came out of Subha's house that day, soaked to the skin in the torrential downpour. As her tutor, could I not have tossed back the same question at her now, so many years later? Why did you not stop me by saying "Don't go out in this rain. You will get wet to the skin." Did you not know I was anyway completely drenched by then?

The Little Carved Box

Translated by **Jayanta Mahapatra**

All the children eyed Mother's little carved box with greed, even Father, among them. It was a small, compact box of rosewood. Inside it was a tray divided into smaller compartments. Underneath the tray, the dark space reminiscent of a lumber room. Strongly built, it appeared like a solid block of wood when shut. In front of it was a narrow hole to fit an iron key. On either side, were ornately carved brass handles for lifting the box. Yes, the box of Mother's was more like her face: noble and wise. Just as one look at her calm, unruffled countenance revealed the priceless, exalted quality of her mind, the sight of the locked box gave an indication of invaluable things stored inside. And just as Ma's face brought on an inexplicable joy, the box filled the mind with sheer delight.

It was Ma's very own box, a part of her dowry. Every bride carried one of these to her husband's house. All other things could be used by the members of the husband's family, but the little box was meant exclusively for her. Some money for her personal needs was kept inside, wrapped in silk. For she would never ask anyone for money when she reached her husband's place, would she? How would she be able to tip the messenger who brought sweetmeats and fruit from her father's house? That itself was an act of honour to her in-laws. There were times too when she would have to hand out little change to the younger ones in the new household, gestures of her affection – again, a mark of honour to her own parents!

And what else was there besides this, which the newly-wedded bride could spend of her will? Just that little box she could call her own; and which seemed to whisper confidence into her ears all the time. For in reality, the daughter-in-law of those days stifled both the inadequacies of her father's house and the indignities of her husband's family – holding herself back, going through life without uttering a word like the little locked box, as her own mother had, in the past.

Ma never let the key to the box out of her hands. Even when death overtook her and she lay in her bed, the worn long key was tied to her sari. At that time, the eldest daughter-in-law had boldly removed the key before Ma's body could be draped in a new sari; her throat dry and her heart thumping away in fear even as she realized that her mother-in-law lay dead; and amid a gripping disquietude that the corpse's icy hand would fall suddenly upon her own and wrest the key of the cherished box from her fingers. And how the eldest son stood there staring like a lump of wood, his heart torn in grief, while they removed the jewellery from Ma's dead body, one after another. There was no other way but to obey the cruel rules of the world. For would Mother ever know that her gold jewellery was burnt with her on the pyre?

When it came to the tiny nose stud they had seen on Ma's face from the time they were children, and Uncle ruptured the tender flesh as he used some force to remove it, an indistinct cry of pain had escaped from the eldest son's lips but he quietly controlled himself. The younger son had in the meantime slipped out of the room, held back his sobs and showed how tough he was. But when the eldest son's wife began to untie the precious key from Ma's sari, tears started rolling down his cheeks and he protested weakly, "Let it be, Rekha. Tie the key back to Ma's new sari. Let it burn along with Ma on the pyre. She had never allowed us to touch it when she was alive."

And Rekha, in a consoling voice, had whispered to her husband, "Don't be stubborn like a child! You'll throw away the key on the pyre, but you won't throw the box, will you? Who knows what the box contains? Perhaps the savings of a lifetime... you know how very thrifty she always was!" And Rekha broke down into tears as she recalled the virtues of her mother-in-law.

But barely two days had passed after Ma's death when they were all concerned as to who would open the box. Who ever knew what valuables Ma had stored inside, but there she had lain withering away to the last day of her life because of Father's indifference, not spending a single paisa on herself. She didn't even disclose what she had left behind for each of them. Certain that the lamp of her life was going out, they had urged her, "Do you have anything to say, Ma? Anything, whatever you wish! Any wish you would like to be carried out?"

But no, like her little strong box, conforming to tradition, she had kept silent. She never said anything before she died. Just before the end came, she held on to her eldest son's arm and mumbled, "My box..." The rest of her words were unclear. Ma's mellow voice had floated away to the other side.

It was however true that Ma never wanted the key to her box to fall into Father's hands after her death. That in spite of Ma's continuing respect for Father, her devotion towards him, the affection called love was not there – all her children knew this very well by the time they grew up. They had come to realize that it was not Ma's failing; on the other hand, Father was fully to blame. That Father had no particular liking for Ma even when she was young, was not unknown to them.

Ma slaved like an ass, and with the limited confines of Father's income saw to it that her five children never experienced any sort of want in their lives. Father would merely hand over his pay packet to Ma at the end of the month; then, from the very next day go on demanding money from her for his extravagances. Ma kept persisting, "Look, there's no more money. I have to borrow now and then to run the house. Have you any idea how much you have taken already? Will the children starve in the end? Here, you look after the household expenses and spend as much as you wish."

The children had got Ma's words by heart after a while, for they knew that after her harangue, Ma would finally open her box and place the few rupees she could spare into Father's outstretched palm.

Whenever the children pestered her for some pin money, Ma groused, "What! Do you think your father is a millionaire! As if he gives me stacks of money month after month, so the children and their father could spend as they liked! Here, hack my limbs, and sell them!"

And the children realized that Ma was only venting her anger against their father even when she raved at them. They also knew that their mother would stomp her feet in open rage as she walked to her room. Then, she would gently open her precious silk-wrapped strong box with a soft click and hand out small change to each one of them. Sorrowful because she had scolded the children, her face would mellow and soften like the earth after a heavy shower of rain, and Ma would go on to fondle them – a touch, a tender caress – a sad sigh escaping from her like a soft susurration in newborn leaves at the first breeze of spring.

She would then mutter under her breath, "If your father only gave more thought to the home, this money would be enough for our needs. Why would they beg for an extra paisa or two and be reprimanded?" And the children would knowingly linger on to hear Ma's words after they had got their share.

In no time the children would seemingly sprout wings at Ma's sympathetic words and skip off happily to school. In their young minds, Ma's little carved box would assume the form of a never-emptying magic casket. For money always appeared to flow from it; some always there, maybe stuck to a corner. It was Ma's auspicious hand which kept the box filled, as each paisa kept adding up. All the household expenses—Father's lavish spending, school fees, the children's pin money and the expenses for festivals and social obligations – were met from this.

About once in a year, Ma settled down to rearrange her box with great care. It was one of the happiest days for the children. Even at this age it is difficult to forget the delight of that moment. Ma and her five children would sit around the precious box, the light of joy and curiosity in their eyes. As if Ma's box contained all the priceless goods of the world! Tiny metal containers with gold nose studs, earrings, gold chains and necklaces, even hair-pieces and armlets—both small and large items of jewellery which were in use in those days filled Ma's strong box.

Ma polished the jewellery she'd brought along from her parents and stored them with care. She used just the necessary few. She knew it was a dream to be able to make money. Your money should be spent in running your homes well. Save a little for illnesses and emergencies. "There's always enough rice here for us to manage."

In truth, Ma had never made any demands on Father for any of her own luxuries. Nor had she ever asked her well-placed sons for money to spend on herself. Even without Father's earnings, Ma always appeared to have enough, like the goddess Lakshmi. Who knew how much she had saved in that box of hers?

Towards the end, Ma never gave a single paisa to Father. When he demanded some money, she snapped at him, "Where can I get you money? There's nothing in the box. I can't go on begging your sons for your shoddy expenses! Do what you like." And Father would shamelessly answer, "Give me the key. I want to see for myself."

Ma would cry out in alarm, "No. Never! Remember, you dare not open my box after my death! I'll tell the children: they'd rather throw the box into the pyre than let you touch it!" And because of the resentment Father harboured against Ma's box, his ill-treatment towards her increased. Still, Ma refused to hand over her key to him. If Father had found out for himself that the box contained nothing, his doubts would have disappeared. Maybe the chaos would have ended. Ma's stubborn attitude irked the children at times. They felt that her old age was responsible for her seeming obstinacy.

Ma, however, continued to open her precious little box at least once a day. Who knew what she did behind closed doors? But when she opened her door and came out, her sad visage seemed to lighten up with a smile as though water had been sprinkled on a wilted flower. Father would fly into a rage and shout at her, "You ill-bred woman! Go; count your money in secret! Carry it with you to the pyre! Just wait and see whether I don't spend away that money in a single day!"

The children also imagined that Ma was counting out her money in her room. Why else would she open that empty box of hers? Why didn't she give Father the key? And the daughters-in-law inferred that she must have hidden away some valuable jewellery, perhaps some of her savings--which she liked to reassure herself with in her last days. She had never spent any money on herself all her life; and even if she had saved a bit, it was never for herself. Who else would inherit it but her sons?

Ma was not that old. It was her loveless life and Father's persistent cruelty and inconsiderateness which had emptied her entire being. And once she fell ill, she took to her bed, unable to recover till the end. She suffered a brief illness, and then she was gone.

She had overheard the children blaming their father as they talked in low tones around her bed and remarked, "Your father was not always like this. He was a good, kind man. A few months after our marriage, he left the village to work in the city. I remained behind. Finally, when I arrived to live with him, he had changed. Bad company had made him lapse into wasteful ways. He had turned inhuman. As long as I had lived in the village, I was at peace, hearing praises showered on him. That was all – my period of happiness. And then, everything went up in flames."

It was difficult for the children to believe that Father had been a kindly man once, and that there had been some love between Mother and him. They had never observed any such show of sentiment, never known Father to grieve even when she had died.

They had not seen tears in his eyes, ever. His whole being remained as though shut towards Ma, shut in like a stone.

Today the key to Mother's precious little box has upset everyone in the family. Who was to open it? Nobody had the courage to do so. Ma had gone without giving anyone the necessary permission. On the other hand, she had asked her sons to burn her box with her on the pyre. But now, the box had to be opened somehow. Certainly Ma must have left behind some valuables, jewellery and money. It wasn't possible that the box would be completely empty.

Nobody could gather enough courage till the end. Finally, the key was placed in the hands of the eighteen-year-old grandson, the college-going Uday. He was the fittest one to open it, they decided, for he alone as a child had been headstrong enough to open the box with Ma's key – whereas Ma had never given such permission to any of her sons.

Uday slowly opened the box. Inside, a number of containers, holders. The three sons and their wives leaned forward to peer inside. The familiar aroma of Ma's hands mingled with the box's smell entered their nostrils, soothing, soul-filling. But had Ma really left behind a lot of jewellery?

All the containers seemed empty—not even a nose stud anywhere. Uday gingerly felt around the bottom with his hand. There was not even a coin, nothing. What had Ma been doing then in secret? Why was she so stubborn about giving Father the key? Uday searched the corners once again. Resting on the bottom was an ornate brass casket. But what was this inside it?

A letter, folded twice. In between the folds, was the photograph of a young man. The yellowed, discoloured picture clearly showed that the youth must be old by now. Did Ma have a lover then?

Somewhat embarrassed by the disclosure, all of them tried to turn their eyes away from the picture. And the sons began to wonder whether Father had somehow learnt of this—perhaps Ma's only weakness in spite of her many virtues—and therefore went on to ill-treat her throughout her life. Was that why Ma would never give anyone the key?

"A love letter!" The smirk in Uday's voice was obvious as he started reading it aloud. "My heart's goddess, beloved Tilottama! The world is a curse without you…" Uday's father snatched the letter from the boy's hand and in sheer frustration shouted at him, "Get out of here! Whoever asked you to open Ma's box? You've just entered college and you are behaving like an adult! All sorts of important documents are inside. Suppose they are mislaid!"

Uday slunk out of the room sensing his father's helplessness. A knowing smile played about his lips. That unromantic, moralizing grandmother of his was once somebody's sweetheart! He couldn't believe his eyes. Who had been her lover? And she had loved him with such unflinching passion that she had treasured the letter until her death!

Uday's father retrieved the letter from under his wife's inquisitive gaze and was hurriedly pushing it into its envelope when his eyes fell suddenly on the last two lines—certainly because of that irresistible desire to find out who Ma's lover was. The next instant full realization dawned on him as he read the name at the end of the letter, and he turned into a lump of wood. The letter ended, "….I enclose a photograph, taken especially for you. Let all your anger be spent on it…. Your unbecoming husband, Niranjan."

It was hard to recognize Father from the youthful features in the photograph. That one letter from her lover which Ma had clung to all her life as her priceless possession had been written only by their father, Niranjan, enabling Ma to gain her strength from this very possession to live out her miserable existence. On this photograph of Father's had piled up all of Ma's anger and pain and wounded pride. That single letter penned by Father to Ma when she was left behind in the village and where he expressed his love for her, was her saving of an entire lifetime, momentary like the fleeting touch of spring. Indeed, how deep was her love for Father! So rare to see these days was Ma's love for Father, something that was sorely missing in his own life.

The, eldest daughter-in-law's eyes turned moist as she looked at her husband with a new-found comprehension. What other priceless gift could have Ma left behind but this – the gift of this knowledge that she had given everything of hers to her husband, loving him till the very end without getting anything in return? Had she herself been capable of such love in the years together with her husband?

Rekha couldn't suppress the sobs which engulfed her whole being as she recollected Ma's unwavering devotion.

The next day the eldest son handed over the key of Ma's box to Father with a straight face. It appeared as though Father had been waiting for this all along. He strode light-heartedly into Ma's room and swiftly shut the door. He had been muttering to himself, "The mean woman that she was, skimping all her life, what did she carry with her in the end? I'll empty her hoard in a day!"

There came to their ears the sound of a box being opened. Then, all was silent for a while. Suddenly, drifted in something new, the sounds of Father's uncontrollable sobbing. The heart-rending cries of a child! "Tilottama, I am inhuman, barbaric! I failed to understand you. I robbed you of your happiness, never giving you anything in return. How will I live, Tilottama? I don't want to anymore!" And in Mother's closed room Father broke down over her opened little carved box.

Eyes flushed with tears, both sons stood near the door listening to the language of Father's finally opened heart. Like the opened box of their long suffering mother after her death, Father's heart had loosened out at last. But Ma was not there to see it. She had left behind the world she had built with her own hands—her own precious box—and gone, gone far beyond all hopes and desires.

■

Antique

Translated by **Bikram K Das**

Ripe mangoes both - the old man more than ninety and the woman probably over eighty. Who could tell when a gust would shake them off? Which one first and which next? That was all that concerned the couple. The man, being older, could be expected to go first. But wouldn't that be unjust to the old woman? Was there anything more they could wish for at their age? God had given them everything: sons, daughters-in-law, daughters, sons-in-law, grandchildren, all the material wealth they needed. Only one prayer she had: "God, let my old man remain. His horoscope says he'll live to be a hundred and twenty, so why can't it come true? Let my corpse be carried out of this courtyard to the beating of drums." Others might pray for long life, but it was death, the old woman prayed for. If God became stingy in granting her wish, who could she complain to? Even that desire remained largely unexpressed. She knew wishes were futile. Is God sitting up there with ears open, waiting to grant your prayers? Besides, what would the old man gain if he lived as long as she wished? Who needed long life? Age was the greatest agony.

The ancestral home was older than the man or the woman - but it was needed. No one would wish it to collapse just because it had stood for a hundred and fifty years. The house spelt security and material benefit, but the old couple meant only trouble and expense. That was the way of the world - why should they have regrets? Both had had long lives; they were probably the oldest people in the village. Most others of their age had gone and they were prepared to go too. Would Death come asking: "Are you ready?". Why bother to prepare for death in that case? Better to live as if there was no such thing!

And, in truth they were not bothered. They lived from one day to the next, sucking the sweetness out of life. They were still able to look after themselves. There was no hassle with cooking; the food which had first been offered to the deities in the family shrine and later sent for them was enough. Besides, at their age, the stomach was perpetually at odds with food of any kind. They ate like birds, just enough to sustain life. Everyone knew they lived contented lives. They never made demands on sons, daughters-in-law, daughters or sons-in-law, asking to be looked after. Let them come if they want to; let them stay as long as they wish. The old lady was not going to send out urgent messages for help at the slightest twinge of pain. Of course, being a woman, she did sulk at times. "Why does one have children? So that they can be a support in your old age, isn't that so? Couldn't they write occasionally? "

The old man would cut her short, saying "Look, it's God, not people, one should depend on! The children have their own lives to live. Will our ailments vanish if we write them ten letters a day? If they did come more often you'd start complaining. Are you strong enough to cook ten kinds of curry for them? Believe me, this is best. It's just like a woman to sulk and moan."

The old woman would spread out her lips in a toothless grin when she heard this. The old man's remark was not an accusation but only an index of his affection. An occasional display of sulking established her right as a mother and wife, and the old man acknowledged that right through his apparent accusation.

The family home, once known as the palace, spoke of their aristocratic roots. It was in a run-down condition now. But Time is less cruel to lifeless objects than it is to human bodies. Although the house had been neglected for more than fifty years, it had not suffered as much decay as the old couple; while their condition became more pitiable with each passing year, the house seemed to grow in splendour. It had a history. Years ago, a Bengali landlord had dispossessed the old man's ancestors and became the owner of the house under the "sunset law"* promulgated by the British. Later, however, when Odisha became an autonomous state with its own language and the alienated parts of the province were re-united, the landlord decided, for some unknown reason, to return to Bengal. The property was put on auction. Fortunately, a member of the dispossessed family put in a successful bid and the palace was restored to its previous owners. So ran the legend.

It was family pride that had brought the owners back. Each brick, each artifact that the house contained, had been a symbol of the family's dignity. It was not possible, therefore, to sell, auction or give away any of the family heirlooms, many of which were now moth-eaten and ruined. They lay scattered about the house in disarray. Who was there to care for them? The objects that had once enhanced the opulence of the home now gave it the appearance of a garbage heap.

To the new generation, these ancient, rusted objects represented an obsolete way of life that was now in decay. Let them think what they please. Who could help it? The old couple had neither the resources, nor the strength to furnish the home with modern contrivances. Each utensil, each stick of furniture was to them a page from the family's chronicles. They could not dream of discarding them. Their bodies too had become ancient and worn out, but would one part willingly with one's body? When the body aged it became home to a million infirmities, but even then it was cherished. On the other hand, those ancient artifacts and implements caused no botheration. They were meek, innocent objects, making no claim on you. They had once served the family's needs, suffered abuse and neglect. Today they were unwanted. They lay smothered in dust and cob-webs. But, they were still dependable. You could sell them off as scrap if you wanted to, use them or give them away. They never interfered with your plans. Human bodies turned frail With the passing years, fell prey to a thousand diseases; but the ancient beds, boxes, trunks, almirahs, cauldrons, water-pots, mugs, spittoons, betel case, betel-nut crackers, spice-grinders and vegetable-cutters, lamp-stands, prayer-gongs and conch shells - they were all ready to serve the family's needs. The old palanquin which had carried brides to their new homes lay unwanted and forgotten on the front verandah. Now every bridegroom, even in the remotest village, comes riding in a taxi-cab or at least an auto-rickshaw.

Human beings were so much more impermanent than lifeless objects, than even bubbles of water. The household goods, which bore the touch of generations, still seemed alive. If one listened carefully one could hear the laughter and tears, the songs and narrations that emanated from them. If one touched them one could feel the shiver of joy as well as pain. Behind eyes covered with the film of age one saw the sparkle of childhood and youth. The celebration of life, the intoxication as well as the imperfection and incompleteness, the futility. Here was the history of not just individuals but of a tribe. The lonely house would echo to the sounds of the past. The old couple, each in their own way, carried on silent conversation with those voices, listened to their accusations, offered explanations, paid homage and sulked in complaint. Why don't you vanish mysteriously one night? How long will you stand guard over us? And when we are no more? You'll fall prey to thieves, won't you? Turn into ashes. Who'll protect your dignity? If your own children can't be bothered, who..."

Is Time to blame? But does Time even care? It is human nature to lay the blame on Time and absolve oneself of responsibility. Has anyone spent a lifetime without holding Time responsible for things going wrong? It may be Time that turns robust human bodies into wrecks, but human ingenuity makes

Time itself obsolete. If Man did not invent new objects, new fashions, new laws, new songs and dances, the word "old" would not exist! All right, granted that what is born earlier is "old" and what comes later is "new"; but where is it written that everything old is repugnant and anything new welcome?

The children did not even look at those treasures from the past; they had acquired new furniture, new utensils: vessels of stainless steel, beds of modem design, wardrobes and much else. One couldn't even pronounce their names. Well, let them do as they pleased. Could they be any different from their peers? Did anyone eat off bell-metal thalis now? Painfully heavy and difficult to clean. Clattering deafeningly at the slightest touch. The children had bought new utensils for the old couple as well. The old woman found them so convenient to use. A little soap-water and they sparkled. Why waste your strength trying to clean the old bell metal things? The children did talk sense sometimes. But, what would happen to these things when they were gone? When the children came home for the occasional holiday the old couple would implore them: "Please take what you want from the house. Who knows when we will go? Relatives are watching us like vultures; our bodies will not even have turned cold when these things will vanish."

And their children and grandchildren would smile subdued smiles as their eyes exchanged messages. "Who is interested in that junk? Let it lie here '"

Their children and grand-children were qualified professionals, earning huge incomes, in exotic currencies that one had never heard of. What attraction could these old pots and pans hold for them? What were they worth anyway? But, could money be the measure of everything?

These old beds, boxes, pots and pans were inseparable from intimate relationships that were invisible to the eye but touched the heart. They caused pain, but also acted as salve. What could the children know of such things? They changed homes at intervals of four or five years, discarded old belongings and acquired new possessions as a matter of course.

Not just homes. It was said even old husbands and wives were being exchanged for new ones.

Well, their children might have discarded other old belongings, but at least they had not exchanged spouses yet. Thank God. But, to people of their generation, all relationships were for life. The old teak-wood bed, with its rough carvings, was as solid as ever. The old wooden trunks remained where they had been placed. The old palanquin, unusable though it might be, still graced the high front verandah. The wheels of the old bullock-cart, no longer used, stood leaning against the cow-shed. The children could not order that these old things be thrown away; they knew the old couple would feel hurt. The things remained where they were. The children would decide later how to dispose them.

But of late, the children had begun to show a new interest in the old house and its artifacts. If not in the old couple. First, a grand-daughter "borrowed" the old woman's antique necklace of rough gold beads, strung with black thread. Antique jewellery was suddenly in fashion, the old lady was told. Let the child have it! Of what use was it to her now? Then a grand-daughter-in-law took possession of a pair of bracelets, whose ends resembled the jaws of a crocodile. One by one. the old woman's anklets, armlets, ear-rings and necklaces were taken over. Good. Better a child have them than a thief. Once the old woman's grand-children had made fun of her blouses with their scalloped sleeves; now they were reported to be back in fashion. The children took away several of her blouses and old silk saris with great eagerness.

One day her grand-daughter picked up her old brass spittoon carefully in her hands. The old woman had scrubbed it clean until it shone like gold. She needed it day and night; wherever she went her spittoon and betel leaf-crusher had to follow. The thuk, thuk of the mortar and pestle, in which her supply of betel leaves and nuts was crushed into fragments which her toothless jaws could munch, was as unfailing as the beat of the feeble heart inside her ribs. The old man's jaws moved to the same slow rhythm. From time to time the stream of betel juice from the two mouths would dye the spittoon red.

" No, no '" the old lady admonished her grand-daughter. "Don't touch that filthy spittoon !"

" I'm going to use it as a flower vase," the girl said.

"Really?" the old lady said. "Then what will your grandfather spit into ?"

"There are so many old bronze and brass vessels lying around," the girl replied. "That brass pot in which you keep your cow-dung soaked rags to wipe the floor with. Why don't you use that for a spittoon ?"

"Very well," the old man said, "if you are so keen on that spittoon, you can have it. We don't mind."

Whenever the children came home now they made it a point to carry away some old and unwanted object. The huge brass cooking utensils from the kitchen were removed. Why were they needed, the old woman wondered. Probably to cook for wedding feasts. But weren't such things available in the city? The children laughed at her question. "No, grandmother," they explained. "No one cooks for wedding feasts now. There are caterers to supply food. The brass pots will be used to decorate the drawing-room. If I cover the brass pot with a brass plate, I can use it as a table. And on top of that' can place the old lamp-stand. the betel-nut crackers, the betel-case. Old things are in style now."

Slowly, the house was emptied of its relics. The old couple were happy to see their wish coming true. Their home was filled with activity. Earlier, the children had come home reluctantly, once in about three years; but now they returned twice a year often accompanied by foreign as well as Indian friends. The old discoloured house and its embellishments were displayed with pride. The village and its surroundings became attractions. Even the old couple suddenly became objects of interest. They were much photographed, frequently interviewed. How long have you been married? How have you managed to stay happily married for all these years? What is the secret of your health?

The house was lonely again after they had left. The old couple would look into each other's faces and say" How they talk!

Well, at least they seem to be interested in old people! Who cares for people like us now?"

The house had seemed more habitable when it had been full; but now it was like a bald palm tree. Everything had been carried off except the old, high bed in which the couple slept. The old woman's father had got the village carpenter to make it out of solid planks of teak. Four robust legs, round as a well-bred matron's. The carving of flowering creepers around the massive bedposts was like the gold waist-band of an aristocratic mother-in-law; above that was the headboard, with bold carvings of elephants and parrots on a bed of lotus blossoms. In between, like the stripes on a sari, were the planks on which the cotton mattress rested. From the four corners rose, like stout arms raised in a lazy yawn, the poles which supported the mosquito net. As though it was not a bed but a celestial angel, charmed with her own loveliness. Now this bed was the sole reminder of the past, the only companion of their old age. It had never been moved from its place. Let it stay. Who would one talk to if everything was taken away? If the old couple had mentioned this to anyone they would surely have laughed. Do beds talk? What could the old people have said in reply? But could they negate their own experience? Beds, boxes, old furniture, the old house, the Mountain Ebony tree peeping in through the window, the fragrant honey-suckle creeper clinging in loving embrace to the mango tree. the smoky odour of the oil lamp that had burnt itself out after twinkling all evening at the foot of the sacred basil plant, the soot which the flickering lantern had deposited on kitchen walls, the cowrie shells glistening in the mud walls of the birth-chamber in which generations of children had been delivered, the palm-leaf scriptures... could the old couple deny that they talked? What stories could that old bed not have narrated? When they rested their old bodies on its planks they invariably heard sounds, saw sights from the past. Memories swarmed around them, clamouring for attention. Sleep stayed away from their aged eyes, and as they lay staring at the ceiling and the walls, the joys and sorrows of bygone days glowed brightly. This bed, they knew, would be their last resting place.

They were well-prepared. But they felt sorry for that old bed. It would surely miss them! The old woman would sit caressing it with aged fingers, counting her memories like gold coins. When the children had last come home, they had admired the bed. Its enormous size made it distinctive. Twin beds were no longer in vogue; people demanded king-sized beds. But the children said no carpenter in the city could copy that old design. No longer was it a profession that fathers taught their sons. Beds were made to order, not out of devotion to an art. Customers were in a hurry; who had the patience to wait for a year ? Raw hands produced raw work.

The children said this bed was now an 'antique'. A rare, valued object. though old-fashioned and unusable. That was what her grand-daughter had explained to the old lady. The old woman's chest puffed up with pride. Remembering her father, she said" The carpenter made it just as my father wanted it. It was planned five years before my marriage. Two years were spent in searching for seasoned timber. The bed matched my father's taste and temperament !" She sniffled a bit in memory of her father. Her grandchildren roared with laughter." Just look at her! She's more than eighty, and she's crying for her father! Did you expect him to be hanging around still ?"

Today's children - ever marching forward. They might turn around to look behind, but they never stopped. But for old people there was no looking ahead; all they could do was to look back, back - as long as their memories had not faded away from sight.

Ever since she had been told that the bed was an "antique" , the old woman's attachment to it had increased. The old man's respect for his father-in-law's good taste had gone up too. How happy he would have been to know that the bed which had been made to his specifications was regarded as a valued "antique" by their English-educated children, who had traveled over the whole world and were earning lakhs of rupees! Well, at least his soul would be pleased!

The shadow of death hovered over them, but the old couple dreaded the thought of dying with no one around them. How pleasant it would be to depart with a crowd of loving children surrounding the bed! But where were they to go ? In earlier days, their children had asked them to come and live with them, but the old couple had been reluctant to give up their home. Now the house was empty. The bed was all that remained to tie them down. If only the children could carry that bed away, then the old couple would follow. They could die in peace on that bed. But the children never repeated their invitation. Perhaps they had been hurt by their refusal.

The servant-couple that had looked after them were old too now. One day a grandson said, laughing" All of you are antiques!" It was said no one grew old now in the cities. No one lost his teeth, no one's hair turned grey, no one walked with a curved stick supporting his bent back. Toothless mouths did not gape or lisp incoherently. Eyes and ears too did not age. Everything could be renewed. Eighty year-olds walked erect. With proper diet and treatment, people could overcome aging. Surgery was available to replace worn out parts of the body. But the village was full of decrepit old men and women. Antique pieces! In a few years, curious children from the cities would come to the village to see what an old man or old woman looked like!

What a craze there was for antiques! Stone statues were carved by artisans and buried in dung-heaps, to be sold to foreigners as antiques! Torrents of money chased these lifeless antiques. But who had a paisa to spare for the aged people in the village ? Human beings were compelled to turn into antiques for want of proper food and medical care.

On their last visit. the foreign friends who had accompanied their children had photographed the old couple on their bed. One antique on top of another! The photograph had reportedly won the first prize in an international competition. Thousands of rupees for one photograph? These people must be mad! The old couple laughed in amusement.

But for some years now their children had warned them not to use that bed. It was too high. If they rolled off it in the dark and broke some bones, they would never heal again.

The old woman would laugh their fears away. "Look, all of you have rolled off this bed at some time or other," she told them. "Are you any the worse for it ? What harm could come to us ?"

But the children's fears came true. One day the old man fell off the bed. He was immobilized. The children rushed home when they got the news. The old couple were reprimanded for being obstinate. Henceforth, they would have to sleep on the floor. The bed lay unused in a corner. The children did not wait to ask for permission. The bed was loaded on a truck and packed off to the city. It was too dangerous to be left where it was. The old people had been lucky to be let off so lightly; things might be different next time. The old couple were silent. But they were hoping that with the bed gone, the children would surely take them away next time. Surely they would respect an antique! If they had such regard for an antique made of wood, could they disregard a living human antique? Their hearts and souls were tied to the village; they would find it difficult to leave, but what else could they do ? They were helpless. If the children asked them they would agree to go. But two summers passed. The children made repeated plans to come but just couldn't make it. The bed, they wrote to the old couple, had become a great attraction in the city. The old woman asked the old man "If old things have so much respect, why don't they take us away? Aren't we antiques too! "

"Be patient." the old man replied. "Someone who truly values old things will surely take us away."

"And who may that be ?" the old woman said.

"Someone who turns new things into old, but not old things into antiques. Someone who gives new bodies to antiques."

"Very well then," the old woman said. "Let Him take us when he wants to. What choice have we ?"

The old woman folded her trembling hands together and touched her forehead.

The Mango Tree

Translated by **Adyasha Das**

Old Mahikant was computing the age of that innocent mango tree. Each branch was over-laden with bunches of young mangoes. During the swing festival, every year, daughter Prathama had swung on these boughs. Elder son, Adyapran, had religiously celebrated his birthday, each year, in the cool shade of this tree. Not the delicious mango of the tree, but this cool shade attracted him the most. Ayushman, the youngest, however, was greedy for every single fruit of the tree. He had been fond of mangoes since his very childhood. The history of the tree is intertwined with Ayushman's greed for mangoes.

When Ayushman was learning to eat, the bazaar was awaiting the arrival of the baiganpalei mango, a popular variety. On the day of his first rice-eating ceremony, a greedy Ayushman had preferred the mango in brother Adyapran's plate to the milk sweet dish in the new silver cup, served to him. With his tiny hands, he had snatched the mango from Adyaprana's plate. And then Adyapran's unending tears! After that Mahikant bought the choicest of mangoes from the bazaar. But no matter how many mangoes he got, the children always fought among themselves for more. Basumati too was no less fond of mangoes. Before the children even learnt to eat, Mahikant had teased Basumati about the heap of mango skins near her plate. But the more the children's hankering for mangoes grew, the less became Basumati's craving for them. Mahikant no longer saw more than a slice in her plate. She resisted his coaxing. "No. The children will want more later. Mangoes don't suit me anymore." Mahikant laughed silently. He knew that even if he got a basket of mangoes, Basumati's children would still want more and Basumati would no longer take more than a slice. None of the favourite dishes of the children would agree with Basumati's system any longer.

The memories of yesteryears were rolling by, one after the other, in a row.

It was Mahikant's habit to bring Basumati something or the other when he got back from his tours. But that time he had stunned her with his gift; he had chosen for her a tender mango sapling. Four reddish delicate leaves opened outwards. With utmost care, he had carried home the young sapling; with still greater care, Basumati took it from his hands, as though it was not a plant with four reddish leaves but a creature with delicate hands and feet. Not a sapling but a newborn baby, her twenty-one-day-old son, Ayushman. Ever so gently, she planted it in a corner of the garden facing the verandah. She protected it faithfully from the many storms and tempests.

When the children were unwell, Basumati sat up through the nights, dozing fitfully, touching their foreheads. In just the same way, Basumati would sit up, startled, in the middle of a stormy night. What if the tender sapling breaks? She would awaken the servant boy and put up a bamboo support beside it. If insects troubled the tree, if the leaves curled up or changed colour, Mahikant, in consultation with the nearest knowledgeable person, would take necessary precautions. Basumati wanted it that way. Mahikant felt he had given Basumati another child, not just a mango tree; their child, this mango tree.

Like the children, the young sapling had, with the passage of time, blossomed into a beautiful tree, laden with fruits.

The mangoes were unique in their taste. The three children loved them. When they would praise them, setting aside the most delectable varieties Mahikant got from the bazaar, Mahikant felt that they were praising him. And Basumati's eyes were lit up with pleasure, brightening her beautiful face, as if the children had got prizes from the school.

When the children left their small town for further studies, Mahikant often travelled to their hostels with a few mangoes, knowing from their letters how much the children missed them.

Basumati would not eat a single mango. She knew that it was costly to frequently visit the children to give them their favourite mangoes. Even so, if ever Mahikant lovingly put a piece in her mouth, Basumati's eyes would at once glisten, moistening her cheeks. So Mahikant gave up forcing her. With the children away, Basumati distributed the mangoes among her neighbours and was praised by one and all for her loving behaviour. No one ever knew that it was the loneliness of a mother's heart that made her do all that.

This mango tree, how old would it be? The first time it had borne fruit was the year Ayushman joined school. Mahikant distinctly remembered Basumati's happy face as she arranged the mango slices in Ayushman's tiffin box.

Oh, how many long years the mango tree would have lived. Even now, it stood poised before him, decorated with sparkling green leaves, like an attractive young woman. The young mango blossoms were swinging merrily in the breeze, without any worry. In just a few days more, the mangoes would ripen.

But tomorrow, the tree would not be there. Instead, there would be plain ground, in keeping with the changed tastes of the children.

A beautiful lawn would replace the mango tree. A rare variety of cactus would be planted in the corner which once belonged to the mango tree. Elder daughter-in-law Sudatta had a fascination for cactus. Yet, Adyapran had once loved the cool shade of the tree. The cactus would provide no shade. But Adyapran shared his wife's enthusiasm for it, along with Ayushman; Ayushman who had taken a month's leave from his research in America and flown to India during the mango season!

Poor Basumati. She was totally shocked. A fertile tree, and not any anonymous, insignificant tree but the favourite of her children not so long ago. She could not bear to think that it would be felled.

Yet she knew that the tastes and preferences of her children had undergone a sea change. She knew it the day the door leading from her bedroom to Adyapran's was replaced with a wall. And that day Mahikant's mind had gone back to the many memories of when the house was planned.

Such a palatial house, in an exclusive locality on the outskirts of the town, was no mean achievement, a landmark in his life. A great history written in blood and sweat.

No ordinary house this. It had been planned on a massive scale. Three big bedrooms for them and their two sons, a hall that would serve as dining and living room, a guest-room and a library. The house would be furnished with the most modern accessories. While planning a perfect home, down to its last details, husband and wife had frittered away the first few loving years of their togetherness in loans, worries and careful budgeting. That was the time when they could have travelled, visited places, indulged in dreams and fancies. Instead, Basumati's foresight and efficiency ensured the building of the house. By the time the loans and debts had been cleared, the children had grown up, so more expenses and responsibilities. They had also aged, walking along the uneven path of worldly life, confronting its many ups and downs. Time slipped away from their grasp, unnoticed, and the season changed. There was no opportunity to spend a few carefree moments together. The only consolation for the many 'could haves' of life was this big house.

Mahikant had protested having a door between the two bedrooms. He was practical, a man of the world. The extra cost of a door was the reason for his protest. His argument was that a modern design without a central verandah did not require a door between two rooms. But for Basumati, there would be no peace without a door leading to her sons' rooms. She had to repeatedly check whether the mosquito nets were drawn, whether her sleeping children were properly covered. And there was another important reason for the door. When they themselves would have grown old, the children could keep an eye at night. After many arguments, Basumati had the final word. There would be a door, leading from her bedroom to both her sons' rooms. Mahikant remembered how he had teased her that day: "No matter how well you plan for tomorrow, you cannot race against time. Wait and watch. The children might not share our likes and dislikes. They might prefer changes - such as a wall instead of a door." Basumati had laughed off his words.

But Mahikant's forebodings had come true. Adyapran's thought processes had undergone a metamorphosis after Sudatta's arrival in the house. Sudatta felt that the door was a rude intrusion on her privacy, and that in future her children would prefer to have independent rooms. Adyapran immediately agreed with her. That day, Basumati had sulked and complained, "It is natural that now Sudatta will ensure that Adyapran gets a good night's sleep. I am not needed to check up on the details anymore. But how will they look after us when we are unwell?"

Mahikant had a yogi's half-smile playing on his lips. He had calmly replied, "Basu, Adya will need an independent room. His first-born will sleep with the ayah in our room. Like our hard-earned, old furniture, we will be shifted to the small room next to the library. Till Sudatta came, you were in the habit of repeatedly getting up at night to peer at the faces of your sleeping children. If you suddenly felt cold at night, you would go and cover them. If it was hot, you would increase the speed of the fan in their room. If a nightmare woke you up, you would rush to the children to assure them not to be startled. Without doing that, you could never get back to sleep. But Sudatta will never fuss over her children. Her child will sleep in a separate room. That is the healthy way. So, why are you sad that the door is now sealed? In life one has to keep in step with the times. Even you had gone against my mother's beliefs. Mother had selected the front room of the house, leading outside, to do her pooja. She had wanted to worship Father's picture along with other idols and to decorate the room with them. But with remarkable guile, you managed to shift the room for worship to the interior of the house. You had explained to mother that people of all castes would walk into her room of worship with their shoes on if it were easily accessible and that the room needed to be secluded. It wasn't as though she agreed with you. But she made herself agreeable to your idea. One is considered clever if one can adapt to any situation. If you ruminate on the past and become obstinate, time will never retrace its steps. Only you will fall back. We are all passengers in an ever-moving vehicle of time. If you lean out of the window and look back, you will get hurt."

No matter how hard she tried, Basumati could not console herself. She could not bear the new look of her room, just as she could not stand Sudatta's short, close-cropped haircut. Slowly, she was beginning to fail to recognize her own house. The renovation continued every day, in every part of her house. And then, one day, Adyapran's name-plate was put up below Mahikant's, in front of the house.

One day, Mahikant and Basumati were returning home from a quiet evening stroll when Basumati stood stock-still near the gate: Adyapran's new name-plate, his name along with many national and international degrees, was shining. But Mahikant's familiar old name-plate, with the colour peeling off, was not there. Only its blurred outline remained on the wall staring blankly at Basumati. Adyapran saw his mother's questioning look, as he walked up to her, and was quick to offer his explanation, "Father's name-plate was really worn out. I will soon place an order for a new one."

Mahikant had a mysterious all-knowing smile on his lips. That smile seemed to say that there would be no new nameplate. Where was the need for it? Mahikant had himself become worn-out, colourless. A new name-plate would not renew him. He said amiably, "If you get a new father instead of this decrepit, senile version, will your mother accept him, Adya? Your mother is truly old-fashioned. No, I don't need a name-plate anymore. You are my name-plate."

Mahikant's magnanimity made Adya feel like crawling in the dust. Basumati had calmed down. In order to survive, one had to console the mind many a time.

But why would they want to fell the poor mango tree? Basumati could not bring herself to come to terms with this. Despite knowing the certainty of the mango tree's fate, Basumati desperately wanted to believe that the children were merely teasing her.

But they had already begun the work. The tree was tottering. The next morning, a few more chops and it would fall. Basumati was grave that whole day. Only Mahikant could penetrate this veneer of silence. That night, Mahikant had many consoling words for Basumati. Like on previous occasions, Basumati had not argued, had not even sulked. Staring up at the ceiling, absent-mindedly listening to Mahikant's monologue, she kept nodding at all the wrong places. She remembered Ayushman as a child, along with bunches of mangoes, swinging merrily. Ayushman's childhood was so inextricably intertwined with the mango tree. Halfway through his monologue, Mahikant dozed off. Basumati was writhing in an intolerable agony.

At midnight, Basumati was rudely awakened by the sound of thundering rain. It was as if the rain and wind were the jealous siblings of the adolescent mango tree. Every year, unfailingly, the cyclone crept in at this time and vented its anger on the unripe mangoes. The congested boughs, groaning under the weight of the fruits, lost their load in no time. Even on this silent night, the jealous cyclone, like a quarrelsome child, was approaching stealthily. Basumati sat up as though in a trance, just the way she used to when Adyapran's or Ayushman's fever would rise in the middle of the night.

Oh! The tree would be bereft of all its mangoes in this treacherous cyclone. Basumati had totally forgotten that the next day the slain tree would be lying on the ground. Even if the mother knows her child suffers from an incurable disease, can she stop his treatment?

Basumati silently left her bed and went out, as though to put up a fair fight with the cyclone. Mahikant woke up the next morning to a poignant confusion. Outside he saw that the cyclone of the previous night had given way to a calm sky.

But in the front lawn, the cyclone had left behind a heartrending piece of its terrible aftermath. Basumati's child, the mango tree, was lying prostrate on the ground, the boughs, leaves, fruits all scattered and wounded like an unconscious, raped woman. But the most unbearable part of this calamity was the disfigured body pressed under the massive trunk of the mango tree, the two lying in a fatal embrace—the lifeless body of the owner of the house, his beloved wife, Basumati.

The mango tree would have fallen someday. Even his Basumati would have had to bid the final farewell someday. That was the immutable law of the universe. But even now the mango tree appeared like a young woman. And Basumati - all round her badly bruised body, the blood-drenched red soil draped her like the blood-red Banarasi sari of their first wedding night. Her unmoving, lifeless form, like the shy, silent bride of that night, blurred Mahikant's meandering vision.

The mourning crowd gathered outside could only think about the incident as an unfortunate accident. With the excruciating agony of deep guilt, Adyapran was pondering, "This terrible accident, caused by Ma's great attachment to the tree, would make me feel guilty for the rest of my life. Had Ma in her quiet grief taken her own life?" The women of their times, the modern daughters-in-law Sudatta and Supriya wept and thought, oh God, Ma had to pay with her life for a few mangoes. True, the truant kids of the neighbourhood might have stolen a few mangoes that rain-swept night. But why did Ma have to be so greedy?

Mahikant stood, the unaffected yogi, witnessing the preparations for his Basu's last journey. Serene, placid and

Buddha-like, he thought, alas, the calculating children of this machine age! How would you know that a mother would jump into the deep sea if only to fish out her child's toy?

No one understood Basumati the way Mahikant did. This was the best example of Basumati's eternal love for her children; for every reasonable and unreasonable wish and happiness of the children - this was a mother's quiet, unquestioning sacrifice.

They were chopping up the mango tree trunk, to be used in the pyre, the final journey of Basumati. Thud... thud ...

Not tears, but the eyeballs were slipping down from the stone eyes of the old widower Mahikant.

■

The Curse

Translated by **Sachidananda Mohanty**

Pari would not have been an outcast had she not
been addicted to betel leaf. Nor would she have
had an identity without it. In fact, it was betel that
stained her reputation and saved it as well.

When the fifteen-year-old Pari first came to
the house as a bride, she was no addict to paan, the
betel leaf. She was just perpetually hungry.
Whenever she missed a meal, her beautiful face
would turn pale, just as the moon does with the
rising of the morning star.

But why talk only of missed meals? Does
anything happen on time for a girl, especially if she's
also a daughter-in-law, new in the house? Pari would
wake up long before daybreak but could go to bed
only around the middle of the night. She would bathe
early in the morning but had to go without food till
well into the day. She could bear delay in all things.
But when she missed her meal, her face would
shrivel up like a fresh green plantain leaf left near a
hearth.

How can a woman, soft as butter, carry the

burden of life? A girl ought to look like butter, no doubt, but she should be able to endure like a rock; only then can she conquer life. Indeed, if there is anything that a woman can fall back on, it is sorrow, for happiness is ever-deceitful. And hunger (there are so many hungers in life) is the root of all sorrow. It is said that we can learn to control all other hungers by first learning to control the hunger of the stomach. Yet, the hunger of the stomach stays on like a perennial bird, pecking at man from birth to death. Hunger has no respect for age.

"A daughter-in-law cannot be good unless she can curb the hunger of the stomach," said Pari's grandmother-in-law who had experienced various hungers at various stages of her life. Now it seemed as if a thousand hungers had settled beneath the folds of her wrinkled skin. She muttered, "I can never get rid of this damned hunger in my stomach."

But like the mind and the body, our tongue and stomach seem to pair off quite well. The stomach feels hunger and the tongue savours taste. So, to appease the stomach's hunger, betel leaf is offered to the tongue as a bribe. When there isn't enough rice in the pot, one takes paan to stave off the thought of food. But the problem with the bribe is that it turns into an addiction and unless it is there after a meal, the stomach remains half-filled. "Yes, pan is the best friend of both scarcity and plenty," said Pari's grandmother-in-law. "I'd rather push aside my plate of rice but never would I give up my pan."

For Pari, it all started when, as a new bride, her face would shrivel up with hunger beneath her veil, and her grandmother-in-law, Ketaki, would thrust a paan into her mouth, saying, "It will not only add colour to your lips but also excite the mind; not yours alone, but of anyone who sees your reddened lips. It will not only control your hunger but also my grandson, Jadua. If you don't cast your spell well in time, my child, you'll repent later."

Pari began to like paan. She realized it brought flavour not only to the mouth but also to the mind. Her red lips added lustre to her radiant face. To Jadunath, she looked like a true angel, straight from heaven. Pari could not say if her hunger was ended by the paan but her red lips definitely killed Jadunath's hunger. As his eyes stayed riveted on her face, his meals often got delayed. He was reluctant to leave Pari behind and go back to the town where he worked. Jadunath had taken thirty days' leave for his marriage and, like the short-lived winter sun, the thirty days were soon to be over.

But what else could Jadunath do without stepping out of the village? Could he plough the field, grow crops? Could he, like his father, carry those loads of vegetables to the market? Is that how he would flaunt his qualifications of a ninth class failed? Besides, Pari's father would not have let him off so easily. It was only out of respect for Jadua's town job that he had given his docile and delicate daughter in marriage to this landless and half-literate Jadua. No one had ever bothered to know anything more about his job. Hundreds of young men like Jadua went to work in distant towns, but when they came back to the village in their new clothes and new shoes, one could easily tell them apart from the country bumpkins. It was certain that if Jadunath gave up his job and took to farming, even Pari would not have the same regard for him. It is not money that makes the difference between a job in town and agriculture; it is a matter of appearance and demeanour. The fact that the husband works in a distant city or town and people address him as Babu, gentleman, is enough to fill a wife's heart with pride. So what if he is always so far away that she's left constantly pining for him; so what if his town-bought dhoti, umbrella, wrist-watch and cigarettes never make up for the woman's longing for her husband.

Too soon, it was time for Jadunath to leave his village. The husband and wife parted amidst oaths, promises, kisses, embraces and tears. One cannot bare one's heart and show one's true feelings to others. If that were possible, Pari would have shown the world how her heart harboured the picture of Jadunath, etched in blood. Jadunath too would have proved that Pari sat like a queen on the throne of his heart, surrounded by a thousand beautiful women who served at her feet. However, such revelations do not seem necessary at such times and seasons; both of them can clearly see each other's soul. With that assurance, Jadunath goes off to some distant place where women tend to charm all men and Pari stays back in the village amidst a dozen flirtatious brothers-in-law, younger and older.

Our Jadunath is truly effeminate. At the time of parting, while touching the feet of her husband, Pari shed copious tears. That was the sign of her devotion to her husband. Jadua shed tears too! "Pari, my dear," he said, "This life has absolutely no meaning! Is it not much better to stay back here and plough the field? Only a worthless man can leave a wife like you behind and go to the town for work. Tell me, how will I survive without you?"

To console her twenty-five-year-old husband, the fifteen-year-old Pari fought back her own tears and placing a scented paan in his mouth, said, "Even if my body is left behind, my soul will always be with you." Perhaps Jadunath would have said something too. But he restrained his thoughts and fell silent.

The family members were waiting to bid farewell to Jadunath. The men stood outside the courtyard near the doorway, while the women were at the entrance to the room. The longer the couple took to bid farewell to each other, the spicier was the gossip among the women. Does no one else get married and go out, or is Pari's the only beautiful face in the village? This was truly embarrassing! What would people say? The auspicious time for departure was nearing, and these two showed no signs of coming out! There was an impatient toot from the bus which stood under the big banyan tree. And the grandmother-in-law called out, "Come on Jadua, your wife will be my responsibility from now on. Don't start spoiling her, child. An excess of lime always tastes bitter, so also an excess of love."

Pari's sister-in-law, who lived next door, said, "Jadunath is delaying deliberately. If he misses the bus, he can stay on for one more day with his moon-faced wife!"

There was plenty of sniggering.

Pari gently pushed Jadunath away. Wiping his nose and eyes with his handkerchief, Jadunath stepped out. His eyes were red like those of the coucal bird. Looking sheepish, he headed straight towards the bus, forgetting in the process even to touch his grandmother's feet. But isn't this the story every time any lovers part?

Pari had no way of knowing how Jadunath would bear the pangs of separation. Thankfully, no one had heard any gossip about Jadunath as they had about the other young men who worked in the town. Jadunath's love for his wife must be the reason. Why were Pari's lips tinged bright red with betel leaf? Why did her eyes shine with kohl? Oh, that's just proof of a devoted wife! So many other women in this village took betel leaf and applied kohl, but how many could boast of such brightly-coloured lips?

Every year, Jadunath came home on a fifteen-day leave. He brought gifts—more for his wife than for his parents and grandmother. At times, there was nothing for anyone barring the love he brought for Pari. No one felt bad about this. After all, the more the son is devoted to the daughter-in-law, the more will he keep away from other women. It is the man who lacks interest in his wife who is likely to lose his way. He wastes money on wayward women and destroys himself.

As for Pari, her devotion to her husband was absolute. No one had ever seen her with her head uncovered or behaving disrespectfully. Like a busy bird, she was constantly at work. But five years had gone by since her marriage, and she had had no babies; only a miscarriage. "Pari is delicate," her in-laws said. "She is young, yet. Let two or four years pass. After all, only a healthy and active daughter-in-law can provide elders with grandsons and granddaughters to play with," they reasoned. Pari is rare indeed! They must have done great penance to have a daughter-in-law like her. So, Pari continued to be the centre of every one's attention, just as Jadunath was the darling of the family.

Pari lacked nothing. Even when he could not visit, Jadunath was never late in sending his father money. The mother-in-law would shove five or ten rupees out of this into the hand of the daughter-in-law. "For you," she would say coyly. Pari would ask,

"What do I need money for? After all, what is it that I lack?" And her mother-in-law would reply, "Let it be. Next time a hawker comes, you can buy a few things—face-powder, comb, hair clips." But Pari spent most of the money on betel-nuts and cardamom; the vermilion and red dye that Jadunath brought from town lasted her a long time. No one had seen Pari lack anything and that, said everyone, was God's grace.

Nor was she wanting in matters of chastity. The very sight of men of her brothers'-in-law age made Pari turn her face and walk swiftly away. It was as if Pari's tinkling anklets posed a challenge to her many brazen brothers-in-law. No one ever dared to joke with Pari. With a husband who was a wage earner and devoted to his wife, why would Pari care for anyone else? She had no hunger—neither of the stomach, nor of the mind.

You may say, a husband who works in a far-away town can send money every month and can take care of his wife's many visible needs, but what of her other needs that lie hidden from all eyes? Whoever keeps track of such needs of a woman, of her restlessness? These can be a source of such embarrassment to a woman, since they can be neither seen nor shown.

At times, Pari's mind did turn sour. When, after the day's chores were done, Pari sat down in the verandah at the back of the house, she was overwhelmed by the intoxicating smell of the atta flours. In the deserted courtyard, with the cool breeze on her face, it was as if she alone could smell those flowers. The champak tree remained stunted. What unknown sorrow weighed it down, Pari often wondered. And then, as if in a dream, she saw the barren branches bear tiny, tender buds. Soon bunches of little flowers would reveal their smiling faces. Isn't the human mind like the champak flower? Chaste white like a saint and within it a hidden, colourful core.

Such thoughts often intensified Pari's loneliness. Would her longing disappear should Jadunath choose to stay back at home? Who could say? There were so many married people in the village. Their quarrels began right from daybreak. Women usually came crying to Pari. "What happiness is there in our lives?" they asked.

"We are no better than cats and dogs. We must be prepared to eat, breed and wait the whole day, all decked up, to satisfy the hunger of a husband. And all because he's feeding you! You're a lucky one, Pari! Your husband is a city man. A real man. He is no rustic villager or an idiot like the others! But happiness is a matter of destiny. There is simply no point in our getting upset!"

Pari was quite content and proud to hear such praise about her husband. But this hardly removed her inner disquiet. Pari wondered if she should tell them of her frustration. Perhaps she would feel relieved by opening her heart to someone. There are so many sorrows that one takes to the funeral pyre, so much gleam that can never be exorcised. It is easy to cut one's blue veins and reveal dirty blood but no one can tear open one's chest and reveal the wilderness within.

Jadunath was not able to come home every year as before. He was entitled to fifteen days' leave every year. But this is of hardly any use. It took him four long days of travel to reach home and the fare was no small amount either. Everyone agreed that by travelling once in three years, one could save the fare of two years and stay comfortably in the village for one and half months. Is it not rightly said that one slogs abroad for the sake of the stomach, even if this is an ordeal?

Pari's world comprised a little backyard, a patch of garden, a pond and trees. A lot of things happened within this world: seasons changed, flowers blossomed and fruits ripened, birds grew wings and flew away to some unknown sky, the mongoose pair enacted its playful game, the bumble-bee alighted on flowers and the snake raised its hood and hissed before slithering back into its quiet pit. In this little hidden world, Pari did not count days; it was years that she counted. Three long years! If Jadunath had merely lifted his head, he could have seen the flowers and the sky and the birds and the snake. Why didn't he? What kind of a man was he? Was he blind or was his heart stone?

Pari sat, a number of thoughts crowding her head. The southern wind blew her sari off her head, revealing her bare back and beyond the heavy fence, a shadow stirred. Pari was startled to see her elder brother-in-law. She quickly covered her face with the end of her sari.

Jadu and his brother were sworn enemies. Nor were the wives on talking terms, as if the quarrel dated back to their previous births. Even the small opening in the fence that divided the two houses had been blocked by Jadunath's father. Nonetheless, Kunja, as Pari's elder brother-in-law, deserved to be respected, even if the brothers did not speak to each other. Yet, Pari wondered what Kunja did every afternoon in the backyard.

Kunja owned a cycle repair shop in the village market, where he earned some easy money every day. He was perhaps the only person who lived well in that area. Older than Jadunath by seven or eight years, he lived in style and God be thanked for that, for who would otherwise have looked at his dark and bony face with the protruding teeth, his tall, ungainly figure? Yet it must be said that Kunja's mass of curly hair was well-groomed, and fell in many layers; not a single strand was ever out of place. He wore a neat set of shirt and pants, chappals and smoked a cigarette. Above all, he chewed pan unabashedly like a goat. To Pari, Kunja looked funny, perhaps somewhat like a joker in a folk theatre group. How often Pari had giggled while comparing Jadunath's looks with those of Kunja! People tended to take this cycle repairer for a city man. But did he stand any comparison to a real city dweller? No wonder, Kunja could never stand Jadunath! Wasn't that what Jadunath had told her? Kunja's hatred for Jadunath had a history that stretched back into their childhood.

Pari usually sat long hours in the backyard, her back turned to the breeze and the fence which was interspersed with knots of thorny bushes. She found that the places where the hedge was thicker were being haunted more and more regularly by Kunja's shadow. A gap, even a little bit wider than what existed, would have turned the shadow into a real human being. But this would have only led to bloodshed.

Kunja's wife, Tulasi, was younger than Kunja by fifteen years and was a dullard. She had three little children. Tulasi was tied to her household chores day and night. Surely, her mind must be active. But no one had ever heard her talk. A temporary visitor would have thought she was dumb.

In the whole family, Kunja was the only one who could afford a mosquito-net. This had such fine holes that it was difficult to know how Kunja slept. People respected Kunja because he used a mosquito-net while sleeping. This indicated the lifestyle of Babus. For instance, he preferred to eat chapatti and not rice at night, a common practice in the household of higher-ups. Like the Babus, Kunja drank tea not in a glass but in a cup with saucer.

Though illiterate, Kunja always had a fountain-pen in his pocket, like the children of the Babus, the gentlemen. A corner of his shirt pocket always revealed an ink-stain, as proof of Kunja's knowledge of its use. He wore a wrist-watch, but to know the time, he had to consult the passage of the sun in the sky and the lengthening of the shadow on the ground. But then, the Babus sport watches, yet they seldom finish any work on time and everything about them is irregular. Hence they too wore wrist-watches not for keeping time but out of habit. All in all, though illiterate and plain-looking, Kunja had great taste. By his demeanour and manners, he managed to cover up his ugly appearance. As a matter of fact, over the past few days, Kunja had not looked half as clumsy as he usually did.

Kunja's cultivated looks did not affect Tulasi, even when he began to pick on her without any reason. Kunja appreciated his wife's naive simplicity. Yet he would be the first to admit that Pari had an edge over Tulasi.

Kunja had never seen Pari's face directly. As she stepped out of the pond, her wet sari clinging to her body, she often saw Kunja breaking a twig from the tree near the fence to improvise a toothbrush. To Kunja, looking through the little gap in the fence, Pari's figure appeared slimmer and more tempting than Tulasi's. Gathering the ends of her sari up to her calf muscles, Pari would squeeze out the water. Kunja would noisily clean his tongue and Pari, like a young sun-yellow butterfly, would be startled and hide behind the hollow of the flowering crape jasmine tree.

In this game of hide-and-seek, Kunja's complexion always

appeared dark. Dark males, we are told, have a reputation for manliness. Jadunath was not dark, Pari thought. He is shorter and slimmer than Kunja. His appearance belied the fact that he was a city dweller. The cloak of city culture that Jadunath put on could seldom conceal the smell of his real rustic background. He stood straight as a cow. How could a man ever hope to get on with his profession and household affairs, if he was not manly? The evidence was right there for everyone to see. Jadunath had a job but he claimed that his pay was not enough. Therefore, he could come home only once every three years. Kunja, on the other hand, had a small shop and every two to three months he could make a trip to Cuttack in order to buy provisions. Perhaps it would have been better for Jadunath to open a shop rather than take up a job. This was Pari's assessment of the situation.

All this was hardly flattering to Jadunath.

As Pari remembered her husband in the far-away town, brother-in-law Kunja's shadow somehow merged with Jadunath's, making him in the process shorter than he was. The loneliness of the dead afternoons enveloped the lonely body and mind of Pari even as she spent them increasingly in the backyard.

Once or twice, Pari had asked Jhatua, the ten-year-old son of Kunja, to buy her a paan from the market. Older people might quarrel but children, after all, are loved by all. When Jhatua and Jhampi quarreled at home while Tulasi was nursing her baby, she bundled both of them to the backyard of Pari's house, saying, "Go and listen to the stories that your new aunt will tell you." Predictably, the busy mother had little time for the children. On holidays, the children hovered around Pari.

Those days Pari got addicted to the betel leaf sold in the bazaar. Without it, she felt dizzy and uneasy. Somehow, a homemade betel leaf did not taste as good. The bazaar paan had a special flavour, a unique aroma, even if at times the excess of lime burned the tongue. It was the best remedy for the loneliness of dead afternoons.

On his way back from school, little Jhatua would fetch paan for Pari like the milkman with the monthly contract used to. But unlike the milkman, he would not accept money, for his father, standing in the paan shop, thought it fit to pay for the paan that his sister-in-law ordered. He may have quarreled with his brother, but was not Pari the daughter-in-law of the house?

Pari's heart would beat faster, either out of fear of her mother-in-law or because of the excitement inherent in the forbidden. Initially, Pari had firmly told Jhatua not to get paan from his father. Jhatua however never heeded her request. It was clear that his primary duty was to his father. With uneasy pleasure, Pari fell into the habit of taking the paan offered by her brother-in-law.

The first time Pari took the paan offered by Kunja, it seemed as if her whole body was on fire. She felt a great throbbing in her chest which was strangely delirious. Had she chewed a rotten betel-nut by mistake, she wondered. No, this headache, heartache and unease must be of a different kind. Had anyone sensed her pain? Whom should she turn to now? Man dies and is turned to ashes. There are many things that get extinguished with the body. No one is able to see the red-hot flame within him. If Jadunath did not come home this Swing festival, he must be a real miser, Pari thought, annoyed.

One day, Kunja's mosquito-net was fixed in the backyard. "It's too hot inside," said Kunja to his wife, "From now on, I shall sleep in the verandah. You can bolt the door from inside." Tulasi raised no serious objection. As everyone knew, Kunja had had a tough time finding a bride. He was well past his prime when he got married. Tulasi, on her part, was dark and came from a poor family. As soon as the marriage proposal was made, Tulasi's father felt as if someone had freed him from a grave burden. Now, Tulasi found no compelling reason to pester her husband regarding his sleeping habits. Nor did she ask why he did not want to sleep in the front verandah, where the soothing south wind blew, and instead preferred the cramped quarters at the back. That was clearly not Tulasi's problem. She was quiet like the greenery of the house. The heat was unbearable inside the house. The backyard was full of trees and was cool, thanks to the pond. Perhaps that was why Kunja slept on the back verandah.

But why did Pari prefer to sleep in the kitchen in the height of summer? Pari was timid. She could never enter a dark room by herself, let alone sleep there. At times, her grandmother-in-law slept with her. Whenever Jadunath came home, the old woman slept in the kitchen. But one day, while enjoying a paan from the market, Pari had said to her grandmother-in-law, "You get up at least ten times at night. My sleep gets disturbed and I have a terrible headache in the morning. Henceforth, let me sleep in the kitchen. It's a small room but our ancestors are there. I shall never be scared!" The grandmother was happy that Pari was more confident now. She had been worried. She knew that her grandson was always away in the city and she herself was like an old palm leaf, ready to fall. If she were to die, how would Pari sleep alone? She could not possibly sleep with the mother-in-law. There was every chance that her sari might slip or her limbs may inadvertently touch her mother-in-law. The kitchen was a much better place. The souls of the ancestors resided there and she was bound to feel more confident.

Thus, the old lady allowed Pari to sleep alone. The older one grows, the braver one should get, she thought. The kitchen was a warm place and there was usually a fire in the hearth till morning, enough to light it with the next day. If not, where would Pari go to fetch a little fire? In Kunja's house, Tulasi lit the fire by striking a match that Kunja bought from the market. But in the house of Jadunath, the city dweller, a matchbox was a far-fetched dream. Jadunath was truly selfish. Why did he not understand that a hearth that had died down can never retain a red-hot fire?

At night, when it was still warm in the kitchen, Pari cooled herself in the verandah. At such times, she noticed her brother's-in-law mosquito-net blowing in the wind. Was Kunja inside the net? From afar, came the sound of someone's feet thrashing in the pond. Kunja must be in the pond. The pond was no source of contention for the men. Anyway, can one think of a fence in the middle of the pond? So, only the bathing ghats were separate. The path from one ghat to the other might be slippery but it was definitely not long.

It is said that even darkness has eyes and solitude has ears and when it comes to gossip, even the inarticulate becomes audible. It did not take much time for suppressed gossip to leap from one thatch to the other; and such messages have a way of reaching swiftly from the village to the town.

It may not be possible to come home on leave when one's father dies. But, it takes no time to rush home to verify a wife's infidelity.

The day Jadunath arrived unannounced and got down from the bus, a stunned silence spread through the village. There was plenty of speculation. Would Jadunath's family be ruined, his world destroyed, Pari's life wrecked? What else could be her fate? At home, there was only Pari's widowed mother. She had no father or brother. Who would come to her rescue now?

Needless to say, sensual and envious men are bound to feel a sadistic joy at this turn of events. Mocking at Jadunath's job and his urban finery, they remarked, "Let the blighter continue to work in the town! We peasants may be poor but at least we have family honour!" Similarly, some women of the village venomously exclaimed, "See, beauty is the cause of all misery. Pari may be beautiful but she is a piece of charcoal inside! How everyone fawned over her beautiful face! Mark our words; it's the beautiful face that gets smeared the most. Better for you to end your life, you shameless woman!"

A sense of expectancy stifled the atmosphere. Not a leaf stirred. It was the lull before the storm.

Jadunath could not look at anybody. The proof of the gossip was all there in Pari's beauty. Could such a thing have happened if Pari was ugly and undesirable? And even if it had happened, would anyone have suspected a thing? The matter would not have spread like the smell of rotting fish, from the village to the town.

For once, Jadunath did not bow down before his parents and grandmother. Dropping his bag in the courtyard, he headed straight into his room. He even forgot to remove his slippers. Gently he shut the door from inside. Pari was standing in one corner of the room.

Jadunath said, "What is this I hear? Is it true? Whatever you say, I'll take as the truth. Am I a moron to ask the villagers about my household matters? I am asking you. If the answer is yes, then I'll teach you a lesson, and if it is no, I'll teach the villagers one!"

Pari fell at the feet of her husband like a log of wood, wailing. People heard heavy thuds like the dropping of fruits from the palm tree. Like a demon gone berserk, Jadunath landed many blows on Pari's bare back. There was no sign of pity or compassion. It was as if he was possessed by the devil. Pari could hardly breathe because of the pain.

Outside, everyone was stilled and speechless. They seemed to be waiting for the final destruction, the last phase of the deluge. Surely, not only Pari's, even Jadunath's corpse would be lifted from this house today, for after beating Pari to pulp, Jadunath cannot remain alive. He will surely end his life. But who can stop Jadunath now, and how? What can the stupid Pari now produce in support of her innocence?

Writhing in pain Pari said, "Please don't beat me anymore! Have pity on me. Believe me, it's no fault of mine!"

"If it's not your crime, is it your father's?" yelled Jadunath.

"I confess, but it is all the paan's doing, the betel leaf. God alone knows what intoxicants were put in the paan that was brought by Jhatua. The trouble started from that day onwards." Sobbing bitterly, Pari fell silent.

Jadunath's raised hand, poised to strike, froze in mid-air and fell limply down. His whole body became lifeless. It was as if he had become a living corpse.

Jadua's grandmother suddenly opened the door. Standing firmly before her grandson, she said, "Yes, that cursed paan is the cause of all this misery. That scoundrel had sent paan so many times for his sister-in-law! God knows what that rogue had laced it with. So many times Pari had told me of the effect of the paan, but even an old experienced hag like me couldn't smell anything fishy. After all, Pari is a child. How could she fathom the complexities of the world?"

Jadunath, laden with dust, grime and tears, collapsed beside the pathetic figure of Pari. Pari continued to sob inconsolably, covering her face with both hands.

The old lady said, "Touch the feet of your husband, and promise him that you are never going to take paan from that blighter again. Is there any dearth of paan and betel-nut at home? Oh, what a lot of suffering for nothing!"

Once again, Pari fell at the feet of her husband and cried. They were tears of regret and repentance. There was a total lack of pretence in that crying. Why did I have to lose my balance, Pari moaned, albeit silently. And slowly, gradually, the injured and mauled husband within Jadunath recovered; after all, it was not as if his wife had deliberately turned towards the other man. She had been a victim of sorcery.

A small breeze stirred in the open courtyard. It was cool, wet and sympathetic. A mild whisper circulated amongst the gathering. After all, whoever had not heard of enslavement through paan?

Lucky Pari! She was saved in the nick of time.

The next afternoon, standing near the fence, Pari was heard showering the choicest of abuses on Kunja. There was no reply from the other side. It was clear that a stunned and dejected man was fading away like a shadow. Very soon, even the shadow disappeared.

Many such days followed. Pari's abuses were followed by silence from the other side. Thus, it was amply proved before all that the fault lay not in the character of Pari but inside the paan.

Gradually, Pari's wounds healed. There were no scars. And although the villagers had talked about it in whispers behind closed doors, they too began to forget the episode.

There was no further problem in the world of Jadunath and Pari. Their life of struggle, scarcity, joy and sorrow did not witness even one other conflict involving Pari's past. And as Jadunath looked at Pari, now a mature mother of five children, he admired her prowess.

Initially, despite his resolution, Jadunath was bent on

tracing out the evil magician who had helped his brother to hypnotize his loving wife. But as we all know, it is always hard to find out such a culprit. Usually, one lays hands on impostors. Jadunath, soon realizing that he had neither the time nor energy to find out who that rascal was, took to soundly cursing the scoundrel to some nether world. Thus, it came about that Jadunath's youth, manhood and anger gradually succumbed to time and the identity of the damned sorcerer remained an unsolved mystery forever.

■

The Gentleman

Translated by **Adyasha Das**

A letter, in an unfamiliar hand, always excites the mind with curiosity about the unknown. But by the time Subhada read through the letter, a quiet sadness had enveloped her. Like sepia-coloured adolescent dreams, the words had been washed by the waves of a far-away time. But the name at the end of the letter, like the silver moon in her own village sky, shone in her memory – bright, calm and unforgettable.

God! He had returned from her very door! Not once, but four times! The trusted and faithful guards around Subhada's palatial house had driven him away. Should Subhada punish them? But then they had merely followed Subhada's instructions dutifully.

Nowadays, for no good reason, a lot of her valuable time is wasted. As though she is the only reliable channel to secure her influential husband's recommendations and favours. That is the reason why she is pressured to attend, or address, or be a member of the managing committees of cultural associations, social welfare organizations, clubs, women's organizations, literary meets and so on. They suffocate her with their unending discoveries of her innumerable talents.

Hence Subhada's strict instructions to screen her guests, and only then either usher them in or show them the way out. Subhada's school-going children are also aware of the hierarchy, who is to be entertained in the living-room, who is to wait outside, or who is to be returned from the gate. In keeping with the pecking order, they have proper answers for phone calls too. At times, her children, with their sparkling, commonsensical wit, spin yarns. Subhada feels guilty that the children are being tutored by their mother to lie; but speaking the truth always lands you in unnecessary trouble, what with supposedly awfully busy men finding greater pleasure in whiling away time in others' living-rooms!

But then, did he have to be turned back from her gate! Not once did anyone ask Subhada who he was, whether he should be called in or not .

Through that whole day, Subhada remained anguished, with an inexpressible, inexplicable ache, and without reason was irritated with everyone. He had written in the letter that the last time he had returned from her door was last Wednesday morning.

Perhaps she had gone out? No, she remembered being at home the whole morning. Then why did he go back? Subhada questioned everyone, individually—did any gentleman come to meet her that day?

They all recalled the day and said—no. No gentleman had come looking for Subhada that morning. The few that had returned without meeting her, Subhada had chosen to avoid. But this happened every day. Some people were invited into the living-room. Others returned from the door. Because someone had to return that day, why was Subhada so perturbed? Not once, but four times he had returned from her barred gates—the moment the thought came, a severe sense of guilt spread its serpentine coil in her heart. In her discomfort, she was becoming restless.

There was no one in the house to understand her feelings.

She couldn't waste her respectable husband's valuable time by discussing such trifle matters—and the children would simply laugh it off. How could Subhada possibly explain to anyone, that the person who had time and again returned from the gate of her castle had held a very special position in her heart, long ago.

Subhada re-read the letter. This time the words appeared quite familiar, as though they were emanating from her very own heart.

Subhada, my child,

By the grace of Lord Jagannath, may happiness be yours always. Your welfare, your husband's fame, the achievements of your children, I have kept track of every bit of news and have been happy. Now I am a haggard, old misfit. But despite that, I had walked all the way to your place, not once, but four times—just to meet my Subhada. Once, you had gone out. Another time you were busy with the morning worship rituals. Yet another time your living-room was packed with gentlemen and so you were busy. The last time you were taking your bath. I was prepared to wait. But your people said, "Get off from the front of the gate. Sir is expected any moment. He has been on tour for the last four days and will return today." I stood at the end of the boundary wall for the entire morning. You didn't come out. Your husband returned. A very generous person. His heart is as large as the sky, as open and magnanimous as Mother Earth. The moment he noticed me, he stopped awhile. He took out a two-rupee note from his pocket and handed it to me and said, "Here, old man. Take this. Why are you standing here in this scorching heat? Go now."

I am not hurt that he took me to be a beggar. My appearance and attire do convey this very impression. Rather I am touched by his generosity. I took the note. Otherwise he would have felt bad. After he had left, I prayed for his welfare and gave the money to an old beggar woman on the road. Is there ever a dearth of beggars on the streets?

I had come to you on an urgent errand. Who knows how long I will live? I have one foot already in the grave. After failing in his intermediate exams, my only son relegated his books to the shelf for good. Now he is sitting around idle. With the hope of help, I had come to meet you, four times. But the Lord didn't want it perhaps. How can I meet you? Travelling from village to Bhubaneshwar costs me around fifteen rupees each time. It is truly beyond my means. Everything depends on your reply. Whatever I do, it will be only after receiving your reply. My helplessness has forced me to ask for your help. Please don't mind.

Yours,
Sir

The image that the wheel of time had blurred suddenly became bright; like a granite idol, the image of a solid, dark, huge statue. A round head, wide face, large, unfathomable eyes, a respectable paunch, legs as strong as pillars, a door-sized chest, betel-stained lips, everything put together constituted "Naran Sir". If his appearance was recalled with closed eyes, the image of Lord Jagannath would appear in the mind's eye. Not fear, but respect and affection would brim over.

He always sat with his legs crossed, in padmasana, a yogic pose. Ensconced in his lap, Subhada had begun learning her alphabet. With his able and sure hand guiding hers, she wrote her first-ever letter. He taught while spinning drunken fantasies of stories, showering affection, and making his students laugh. Like a dead, emaciated snake, the thin, lifeless baton remained in a distance. It was never required. The kids were never scared of "Naran Sir"; they loved him, respected him.

When she was being enrolled at school, Naran Sir named her Subhada instead of the original Subhalakshmi. He had said, "We have three favourite deities—Jagannath, Balabhadra and Subhadra. It is auspicious to have a name with three syllables. Moreover, Subhada wouldn't mean Lakshmi, the goddess of wealth alone but also Saraswati, the goddess of knowledge. She would be auspicious for everyone." Father was happy. Ever since, she was Subhada, for everyone. Later, when she was a little bigger, she herself developed an affinity for Subhada rather than Subhalakshmi. Naran Sir had chiselled and moulded lots of other names when entering them in the school register. Each student fell in love with the re-modeled name, just as they all loved Naran Sir above anyone else.

Subhada was the apple of her father's eyes. She did not easily take to people. If her mother ever, in her anger, made the mistake of slapping her, Subhada's sobs would be a never-ending song till Father returned. The moment Subhada saw her father, waterfalls of tears would cascade down her eyes, like the milk that would spurt from an unsuspecting papaya when a stone hit it. The faint memory of the slap would hurt her cheek with renewed vigour, just like hands that burn after grinding red chilli. Father would then caress her cheek, would show mock anger to Ma for unreasonably punishing his darling daughter. Subhada's tears would immediately stop, like fire after a sprinkling of water. With the light ring of laughter on her lips, she would hide her face in her Ma's saree and would say, "Ma, why does Father scold you un-necessarily? Don't take it to heart, hmm, my darling Mama." Subhada was like that, couldn't tolerate a reprimand from anyone, couldn't bear to hurt anyone; a butter-soft mind, like the many-hued, tender flowers of her village grass. A mild touch, and definitely, there would be an imprint. Naran Sir knew about this. Glaring at her wouldn't coax her to study: her never-ending tears would colour her eyes a deeper red than the teacher's glaring eyes. But just a loving pat on the back, a word of praise, and Subhada would not only study but excel in it. Naran Sir would first acquaint himself with the whims and fancies of his students and then teach them accordingly. Which potion would be most effective for whom, which spell would entrance whom—how could Naran Sir be so all-knowing, like God?

Subhada was scared of anything and everything. Unfamiliar faces, familiar village roads, dogs, monkeys, cemetery, vast expanses of fields, the wooden bridge curved over the canal, scorching heat, the dark shade of a bushy tree—everything scared her. When the morning school was over, Naran Sir would walk down with her until the frightening, deserted by-lanes were left behind.

Just beside the school was an old Muslim shrine. The

entwined branches of the spread-eagled tree, like the hands of a great demon, were extended downwards, as though to tear open the very heart of Mother Earth. From the top of the tree, monkeys by the dozen climbed down, screeching, chasing and blocking the road in the middle. At the end of the road that ran across the Pira Sahib was the Muslim graveyard. This road, for Subhada, was as terrifying as hell itself. Naran Sir would hold Subhada's little hand in his own and would narrate the most hilarious stories till they had crossed that road. Then came the hospital. There too, in the heat of the lonely afternoon, fear would grip Subhada. Memories of dead bodies and about-to-die patients would be revived at this point and Subhada would be terribly afraid. Between the hospital and the bridge over the canal, flanking the straight road on both sides were wavy green rice-fields. They too frightened poor Subhada. What if the green waves stretched out and pulled Subhada's toddling feet into their midst and if there were fat frogs, cranky crabs or quarrelsome crocodile twins, what would be her plight?

Naran Sir, walking barefoot and so fast over the hot sand, would say, "Come, I will leave you at the other side of the bridge." Once on the bridge, Subhada would get back her strength and courage. Nestling on the opposite side, the small village bazaar would suddenly seem very safe and secure like grandma's lap. But the bazaar would come only after crossing the bridge. Naran Sir would hold her tiny hand and help her cross the rickety, creaking bridge.

After crossing the bridge, Subhada would say, "Sir, now I can go. I can already see the house. I am no longer scared." Naran Sir would continue walking, with his face downcast and would say, "No, I will walk with you till after the bazaar. So many vehicles are moving on the road these days. If the road is crowded . . ."

Subhada knew as well as Naran Sir that the deserted village road, where vehicles plied only twice daily at a scheduled time, would not become crowded all of a sudden. Nevertheless, Naran Sir would help her cross the bazaar. The massive boundary wall surrounding Subhada's house was at the end of the bazaar. There, Naran Sir would stop near the gate, and say, "Go. Now go home."

On the straight pathway leading from the gate up to the house, Subhada's stride would be a great deal more relaxed. Subhada would fervently wish to call Naran Sir up to the house. There her mother would offer him buttermilk or force him to have his lunch before leaving. But she knew Naran Sir had to take his bath, do the customary worship and only then would he eat something. Apart from tea and betel, he refused to eat anything without taking his bath.

Till Subhada entered the house, Naran Sir would keep standing in the sun, watching, waiting. When Subhada sat down to eat, she often wondered, why did Naran Sir walk all the way without bath and food , every day, unfailingly; in the hope of what? Naran Sir had never spoken about his problems to any guardian. He never accepted tuition fees, despite spending extra hours in coaching weak students. On his own, for his own happiness, he offered his services as a teacher, offered his affection. Is the value of that so little that he can actually ask for it and get it? Naran Sir would always say, "Your parents want to make you goddess Lakshmi, the goddess of wealth. But I want to see you as Saraswati, the goddess of knowledge. If you are sincere in your studies, you too can become Saraswati. You will be the pride of this entire area." Today, whatever Professor Subhada has achieved, wherever she has established herself, Naran Sir has a significant contribution to it, this Subhada has realized time and again. Whenever Subhada's mind wanders back to those dog-eared, yellowed days of sitting comfortably in Naran Sir's lap and studying, Naran Sir's face in her mind merges with Lord Jagannath's. Subhada, with deep respect in her heart, offers her regards. She thinks that each time she offers obeisance to Lord Jagannath, Naran Sir receives it. "Guru is Brahma, Vishnu and Mahesh" was probably written, keeping Naran Sir in mind.

The same Naran Sir, what help could he possibly want from her, for which he had to return four times from her gate? It's not strange for Subhada to expect relatives and even acquaintances to approach her for help in different fields. The world thrives on mutual help and cooperation. At times, even Subhada needed help from others, even if it was in the form of a mere word. But it really hurt her that Naran Sir, at his age, had travelled all the distance from his village to Bhubaneshwar for some help. It surprised her as much as it hurt her. Probably, it's true people change when in need. Naran Sir was old, unemployed for long. The son was totally useless, a loafer—a load, a heavy burden on him. Probably, he intended to request her to find some means of employment for his son or perhaps to ask for a loan to set up some kind of business for him. If it was within her means, Subhada had always been more or less helpful. She had few friends, more enemies, because it was not always possible to help everyone. Her magnanimity, inherited from her mother, was reflected in her sincere desire to help those in need. For this, she had herself faced many difficulties at times. Nowadays, Subhada thought twice before helping anyone. In fact, for this one thing her husband and children were frequently irritated with her.

Subhada thought helplessly, oh, why did Naran Sir demean himself by asking for my help, just like any ordinary person? Nowadays, for whosoever came to her house seeking help, Subhada has developed a dislike. For those who got help from her very often became her critics and even her enemies. But if it were not a genuine problem, Naran Sir was not the sort to request anybody for help. Subhada became restless. Because she couldn't meet Naran Sir, she snapped at everyone. Ultimately, she found out that her youngest son had been instrumental in sending "Sir" back. But then, how could he be held responsible? That day, the moment Subhada opened the tap for her bath, her youngest son had banged the door, "Ma—someone is looking for you."

"Who?" Subhada raised her voice above the sound of the running water.

"I don't know," her son shouted back, louder.

An irate Subhada snapped, "Why don't you ask who it is? What work does he have with me?"

The son retorted, "Whenever I ask that, he keeps insisting that I call you, 'You are a kid. How will you know who I am?' "

In her haste, the soap on her face spread to the eyes. The more her eyes burnt, the more irritated she got. Surely, some enemy in the guise of a friend had arrived. This sort of a reply was typical of them. Subhada once again asked, "Is he a gentleman?"

"Oh no, not at all a gentleman," Subhada's son replied promptly.

This time Subhada yelled back, "In that case, simply tell him, 'Ma's taking her bath. She will be late. Come later.' Why are you irritating me? Can't I take a leisurely bath even on a holiday? Haven't I said if it is a gentleman, call him into the living-room? Otherwise show him the door."

Subhada opened the shower and washed her head till she felt cool inside. Her obedient son asked the old man to return from the gate.

The angry Subhada continued muttering under her breath, these children—what's the good of studying so much if you can't distinguish a gentleman from a common person. Hmph, if Naran Sir was not a gentleman, no one in this world could be one.

Her youngest son was silently ruminating, "Do you really recognize a gentleman, Ma? All the so-called gentlemen you invite into your living-room are involved in ungentlemanly acts. Some request Professor Subhada, with the roll number of their children or relatives in hand, to increase their marks in the exams; some come to flatter Father for an undue favour. All these beautiful people, under their gentlemanly masks, are corrupt. They should not at all be called gentlemen."

Overtly, he said, "How do I know who is a gentleman? That old man was in tatters and was so dirty. He should not have even stepped into the living-room."

Subhada was helplessly thinking, truly, who is a gentleman? What is the true definition of one? What could she tell her son? How could she explain to him that even the dust of his feet in her living-room would have washed off her many sins.

Despite all her respect and affection for Naran Sir, a worm

was stealthily eating into her thoughts about him. Naran Sir too, like everyone else, had to ask for help? If the extent of the help he sought exceeded her limited means, would she then become an enemy? Would he curse Subhada?

In thinking about how to send a proper reply to Naran Sir, she didn't write back at all. What if she promised help and later proved incapable of keeping her word? Naran Sir was not just anyone that she could make false promises and not feel the least bit remorseful afterwards. But if she didn't assure him of help, what could she possibly write in reply? Who knew how much he expected from her? Like bargaining with the shopkeeper—on the principle that if you ask for twenty-five, you get five—even help is bargained for these days. Was Naran Sir asking for some unreasonable assistance? Who knew, nowadays, his condition was truly deplorable. Subhada had heard that he didn't get enough food, let alone medicine. Thinking about this and that, about what she could write, Subhada remained silent for many days.

Suddenly that day, a registered letter arrived from Naran Sir. Her husband and children sarcastically quipped, "There comes your reminder. Just in case the appeal for help gets lost, it has been registered this time. Now there is no excuse for you. After all, he helped you write your first alphabet. First, just check the amount you owe him by way of your gratitude."

Subhada, in her unhappiness and remorse, went red in the face. She eagerly opened the letter. After reading the letter, she was stunned. Her education, culture, wealth, status, everything was stripped off by that one letter. Nabin, Naran Sir's only son, had written the letter.

Respected sister,

Fifteen days back, Father expired. Till his death, he was constantly remembering you. He was hoping that after learning about his four futile attempts to meet you, you would definitely come running to the village to meet him, at least once. If nothing else, at least a letter from you, promising help—that was all he expected. If only he had received that letter, he could have at least died in peace.

Sister, Father couldn't repay a loan before dying. That was the only cause for his unhappiness. When my younger sister got married, your father had forced Father to accept two thousand rupees from him. Had it not been for that money, the groom would have returned without the bride. Though your father considered that money to be a gift, Father took a pledge to repay it. But I was an inefficient dud. Who would repay the loan? In the meantime, your father too expired. But Father didn't forget the burden of the loan for a single moment . How he could return that amount to your brother was his constant preoccupation. That was why he had gone to you. In Father's calculation, two thousand rupees then, along with interest, would amount to more than ten thousand now. So, apart from this house, which he left to me, he has left his entire property for you, in your name. Either you keep the property and give an equivalent amount to your brother or sell it off—whichever suits you better. It was only for this that he had been to your house, despite his illness and pain. The village folk, taking advantage of Father's helplessness and my inefficiency, wanted our golden land for peanuts. Just for these problems, Father couldn't sell off the land earlier and repay his loan. Otherwise he would have died a peaceful man. In the absence of your letter, he left this world with a big burden on his chest. Please forgive him for any trouble you might have had to face; he pleaded for it while dying. God be with you.

Unfortunate,
Nabin

In Subhada's assessment, Naran Sir's property was worth much more than ten thousand. Why did Naran Sir gift her such an insurmountable burden of guilt and grief? Probably he did this because of his love and implicit trust in her.

Subhada had cried like this once, after her father's death, as she was crying now, inconsolably. But today her tear drops were blood-red. That day she had become blinded with tears; today the agony of her heart was raining through her eyes as blood.

■

The Other God

Translated by **Sachidananda Mohanty**

They had set out in search of God. They knew they would not find Him unless they put aside their doubts about His existence. They had no important business with Him. They were not in need of anything, so they had no favours to ask. Curiosity had led them to this search. They had come to India first for they had heard that if one had true faith and sincerity of purpose, one could meet God there.

God is not a debatable subject. If one is in a quandary about his existence one cannot have faith in the quest. So the two foreigners first visited various saints, holy men and seers to find a spiritual master who would allay their doubts and guide them in their paucity of impostors and cheats.

Disillusioned, the duo then visited temples, mosques, churches, and other places of worship, hollows of trees, ant hills, mountains, and caves in search of God. Their efforts were in vain.

The seekers were rational beings. Their beliefs were based on reasoning and logic. They knew that statues made of wood, stone, gold, silver, marble and bronze, or painted pictures were not God because they were perishable. Also they were man-made. Then they thought that God-realization was antithetical to logic and argument, so they tried a different path. They encountered many scholars. Finally one convinced them that devotional worship, God and logic were not opposed to each other. But their search would be futile if they followed blindly the path pointed out to them.

They accepted him as their master and questioned him, "What color is God? What is his shape? Have you seen Him? Felt Him? If not, how can you believe in His existence?"

Eliciting an answer from the disciple rather than giving it to him is the mark of a true master. Matter-of-factly, the master countered "What is light?"

"Energy" replied one of the foreigners spontaneously.

"Have you seen light? Is it visible?" asked the master.

The foreigner thought for a moment, then said, "No. Light itself cannot be seen. It only helps us to see other things."

"What is the color of the light?"

Flustered, the foreigner answered, "Light is white. No, no. Its blue… green…red … dark like Krishna. pink… yellow….No! Light has no color. It does not possess any color, but it lights up the color of objects by reflection."

The master smiled. "When is light present – at dawn, noon, dusk or night?"

This time, the foreigner's reply was quite emphatic. "Light is present at all times. Those who think that light is not present during the night are ignorant about the properties of light."

A light seemed to descend on the master's face. "Does light have a home? Does it belong to India, England or America? Does it live in space, on mountains or in the seas?"

"Light is not confined to one place. It is present everywhere. It transcends space and time. It is neither in America nor in India.

To say that light belongs to a particular country or community is supreme folly," answered the foreigner categorically.

Smiling enigmatically, the master asked, "What is the path of light?" "What path does light follow?"

The foreigners must have been scientists. "Light passes through pre substance. It cannot pass through opaque matter", one of them responded.

Gradually a light illuminated their faces.

"Have you touched light? Is it smooth or rough? What is its shape?"

"No. I have not touched light. It does not have a definite shape."

It was the last question. "So how do you know that there is something called light?" queried the master.

The foreigner was quick to explain, "Light is an experience. The realization of power comes only when you experience it."

The master was pleased. "Friends," he said, "you have answered your own question. I believe your doubts about the existence of God have been dispelled?"

"How?" they asked, still confused.

The master patiently explained, "God is a power like light. He cannot be seen Himself but makes everything visible. God has no shape. He can only enter a pure heart. He is present everywhere and is not bound by space or time. Just as the world is dark without light, without realization of God, man's consciousness is clouded by illusions. God is a matter of realization. His extraordinary power can be felt only when man's thoughts rise above the mundane. He is visible in a highly refined form that is beyond thought and consciousness. The cardinal principle of wisdom is this quest for pure truth and unalloyed happiness, which reveals that God is light and salvation, aspiration and realization."

The foreigners analyzed the master's definition according to their knowledge of modern science, their wisdom and intellect. He had told them many other things about God. But he had not revealed to them the secret of where and how to find Him. Of one thing they were convinced - that God is omnipresent. So, getting rid of all further doubts and apprehensions they embarked on their search, confident that He would appear to them if they were persistent and had unshakeable faith.

During their travels the two foreigners encountered many people who claimed they were God and resorted to fighting, bloodshed, hatred and deceit in their effort to prove it. They assessed all of them in the light of their master's description and analyzed each 'god'.

"Is a scientist God?"

"A scientist is an inventor, not a Creator. He cannot be God."

"Then is an artist God?"

"An artist does not create; he merely gives form to the beauty of Creation."

"Is a master God?"

"God is the supreme master"

"Celestial deities, both male and female?"

"God has no gender, no sex"

"Ancient beings are God?"

"Is a king God?"

"A king's throne is not his – it is only a temporary boon bestowed on him. A king may become a pauper in course of time."

"Then who is God? Where is He?"

The foreigner duo has already toured India extensively without meeting God. At last they have decided to go back home without seeing Him. They are at a railway station, waiting for the train. But the train hasn't yet arrived. They are not unduly worried for they know that this is not uncommon here. They watch the other passengers who know it too but are agitated and anxious.

Actually, today's delay is a bit unusual. A tree has fallen on the railway track due to a storm the previous day. The line is being cleared but almost all the trains are running eight to ten hours late. The passengers learnt of this only after they came to the station. This information could easily have been broadcast earlier either over the radio or on television. Many things which ought to be done promptly are not done here. The result is confusion, tension and chaos. The situation at the railway station today is exactly that.

There's no place to sit on the platform. It's overflowing with noisy passengers, heaps of luggage and litter strewn everywhere. It is best not to speak about the bathrooms and toilets. Each person feels that since he is going to board the train shortly it doesn't matter to him if he throws his rubbish all over the place. And everyone is an expert at blaming the other person. Cleanliness is the responsibility of the railway authorities and the sweepers, not the passengers! The end result is filth and garbage and an all-pervasive stench. This is a regular feature, no doubt, but: due to the unprecedented crowds, it's much worse today. All of them are holding handkerchiefs to their noses and cursing everyone else for the mess.

Those who had got to the waiting room early are sprawled comfortably on the benches and sofas. In one's home one invites a stranger to sit, offers seats to visitors in the drawing room but in a public waiting-room one person stretches out even as another is standing! Simple courtesy demands that one makes a bit of space for another but who bothers about causing inconvenience to another, or respects the other's right to sit, in public places. The general attitude is, "I've come first, and this is my space."

The foreigners were forced to return to the platform. For although it was filthy and crowded, there was still standing room. Some passengers had parked themselves in the comparatively cleaner areas. Some cheerful, rather respectable-looking people had spread out some newspapers and were sitting on them. They appeared to be two families going on a holiday together. Two ladies, two gentlemen and four children, all of them plumper than necessary, their smooth shiny skin reflecting the rich, oily food they consumed. Their bags, suitcases, tiffin-carriers and water bottles looked quite expensive too.

When they saw the two foreigners nearby, their faces seemed to light up. The ladies, chatting desultorily as they reclined against their bedding, pulled out little hand mirrors and began to repair their make-up. They touched up their lips, and reapplied powder over the layer of sweat and grime that had settled on their faces since the morning. All the while watching the foreigners out of the corner of their eyes.

Suddenly, they are no longer tired, impatient or irritable.

The foreigner duo has become a diversion, a source of entertainment for them. Slowly they edge closer to the foreigners.

During their stay in India the two visitors had realized that in the past, Indians were known for their patriotism and were willing to lay down their lives for the country's freedom. Today (who had not lacked a patriotic zeal in the past and were ready to lay down their lives for their nation) are more enamored of foreign countries. Once upon a time, Indians had boycotted foreign goods and freed India from the British. Today, in free India, her countrymen are not only eager to use foreign goods; they almost have an obsession for them. The word "imported" has become a status symbol. Goods considered cheap and useless in other countries are collected by Indians because they are imported. Even today, many educated and illiterate consider foreigners to be messengers of God. They stare at them, bursting with curiosity and wonderment. Beggars believe they are lords of the city of wealth.

The foreigners have already exchanged their pens, watches, belts, jackets, combs, blades, and shaving lotions for their Indian equivalents. What a strange fascination to give new articles for old and used ones!

Wherever a fair skin, blonde hair, blue, cat's eyes and colored lips are seen, curious Indians gather and without bothering to find out from what country they come, they immediately label them foreigners. They get totally swept away by this word and do whatever they can to get close to the foreigners. Some try to extract information about how one can go abroad. Some even try to get information on the way and means of going abroad. Perhaps it is the Indian idea of hospitality. It may be natural to display a fondness for a friendly country.

The family group had almost surrounded the duo and was trying to strike up a conversation. They had introduced a foreign accent to their normal English. It made their speech awkward and incomprehensible. One by one they began to open their bags and exhibit their possessions. They wanted to show that they used many imported goods. They tried to impress the foreigners with their wrist watches, cameras, tape-recorders, VCRs, etc. Then they handed the duo a list of their relatives who lived abroad. Soon there were no doubts left about the status of these two families - they belonged to a higher level than ordinary Indians.

Their overtures of enthusiasm however were not wholly reciprocated. Two pairs of blue eyes were fixed on something, else. Recalling the various definitions of God they had been given, they were keenly observing a rather weird creature in a corner. Perhaps they would really find God after all.

They could see two eyes lying on the platform. Did they belong to the platform or that creature? Was it an animal or a human being? Or was it God?

They had seen this creature roaming about all day. Now, it lay sprawled on the dirty platform, a symbol of grime. During the day, the creature had a porous stained piece of cloth which kept slipping off its waist. But it didn't seem to care. Now it had stretched out, stark naked under the tattered rag, but with the haughtiness of a king. What was the color of its skin? Fair or dark? Once upon a time, there must have been some complexion but now there is no difference between the discoloured filthiness of the platform and the pallor of its body.

One couldn't tell the shape of its face without the cover of flesh, all skulls and bones look alike. Its bones were stretched over with a fleshless layer of skin.

Was it young or old? It was difficult to tell whether it looked skinny because of age or disease, hunger or fatigue. It could have been either.

Minute vermin's swarmed out of the unkempt hair and played around its head. When asked what they were, a child replied, "Lice." Many shelter under one being. Like the soul taking refuge in God, and atoms in molecules.

The creature picked out the lice with its bony hands and squeezed them with the help of its long nails. Creation, preservation and destruction, all embodied in Him.

One hand of the creature is spread out as if holding aloft the torch of freedom. Grime is caked under the long nails. The palms are open, as if signifying "Take everything, give everything."

He who gives and He who takes. Who is He?

The more they observe the creature, the more excited the foreigners get.

They are matching this creature.

God is omnipresent. They have seen this creature throughout the country.

God is pure. He doesn't need to bathe. It is obvious that this creature does not bathe either.

God does not need clothes. Does, Beauty need ornamentation? Such a creature never dons clothes or ornaments.

What is the need of scent for the unsullied? Incense for the scentless? Food for the detached?

Neither stink nor fragrance affects this creature.

Nobody seems to make offerings of food to it.

God does not possess ego, anger 'or arrogance. These creatures are unaware of insults to their pride and prestige. They have no ego, hatred, anger or jealousy!

God is neither young nor old.

God is nameless and yet has all names. These creatures do not have a name either. Leper, cripple, old man or youth, they are addressed by all these names and more.

The foreigners went up to the creature.

"Who are your parents? When were you born? Who is your son, your daughter?

The creature waved its hand, indicating no to every question. It was not aware of its existence, its birth. It had no kith, no kin.

God does not have any relatives! He is free from the hassles of human relationship / all human bonds.

The foreigners asked again, "What is your caste, your religion? Who is your God?"

Again the hand shook. "No, No, I have no caste, religion or God." God does not have any caste or religion.

Who can be the God of God?

So who is this creature?

"Where do you dwell. - in temple, mosque, church or gurudwara?"

"I do not have a house."

God has no base, what use a house to Him?

The children of that group tugged at the foreigners. Their mothers were opening the tiffin carriers and displaying a vast variety of delicacies. They urged them to share their food.

The creature's arms were spread in an all-encompassing embrace.

Throwing a look of utter disgust at the creature the gentlemen thrust plates heaped with food at the foreigners.

The duo folded their hands and apologized, not out of courtesy but out of suspicion and fear. India's food, medicines, milk and water are all contaminated. The polluted atmosphere is full of harmful germs. Eating cooked food here meant certain death. They consumed tested food from well-known hotels and drank only mineral water which they carried. They had brought medicines from their own country with them.

With handkerchiefs to their noses to keep out the foul smell permeating the atmosphere, the group was trying to eat. It was a question of survival.

One of the children vomited into a plate. The stink was nauseating. The lady collected all the left-overs into the child's plate and put it near that creature.

The foreigner duo shuddered. Before they could object, to their horror, the creature emptied the contents of the plate on to the filthy platform and, eyes glittering, wolfed it down, dirt and all, in large greedy mouthfuls.

God can survive without food. Yet He also eats all.

The foreigners exclaimed indignantly, "What have you done, given him leftovers?"

With a contemptuous laugh the gentlemen said, "Nothing happens to him. They don't die. They are not afflicted with disease. They wouldn't survive, propagate and spread if did!"

God is indestructible. He is not affected by sun, rain, fire or germs. He does not die by consuming rotting foodstuff. He reigns everywhere.

The foreigners were so excited, they were almost dancing

with glee. Finally they had found God. The family took photographs of them. They took turns to pose with them.

Then the foreigners produced their camera. All the members of the group were eager be photographed by a foreign camera. "Please send us a copy. We will give you our address," they humbly requested.

Overcome by emotion the foreigners declared, "At times God comes down to Earth in a mysterious way. He reveals Himself to us only after He takes account of our state of consciousness, in one divine moment. Those who lose this opportunity because of ego or ignorance are unfortunate and their destruction is inevitable."

As they spoke they captured God in his most amazing form on their camera.

The gentleman was dismayed. "Why are you wasting imported film on a beggar? What beauty do you find in this diseased creature?" Clicking away rapidly, the foreigners said "When that divine moment presents itself, all sense of false pride, vanity and self-deceit vanish. The devil's voice is sure to distract you at this time. But if you ignore it, in that unimaginable, uncountable and unexpected moment, God in all His glory will be revealed to you."

An instant photograph was emerging from the Polaroid camera. It was quite repulsive. Rejecting the divine moment, the men and women snatched back their outstretched hands.

"One can never understand the mentality of these foreigners." They whispered among themselves. They are fascinated by ugly, filthy beggars. They don't know the difference between a beggar and God. A person who is not born in this sacred country of India can never recognize God."

Animal Birth

Translated by **Adyasha Das**

It is the month of December. The night reverberates with salap, the locally brewed alcohol, drugged by the wine festival. Has the moon been silver-plated or has it been laced with gold? But then, the moon isn't like jail-returned Buda Kirsani, who had to bathe and drink silver-gold sprinkled water in order to be accepted by his kinsfolk.

Moonlit nights enchant, intoxicate and instigate man to kill man. There is no enclosure for the moon but there is one for man. Atop the Bondo Hills, in a step-like fashion, thirty two villages nestle, one higher than the other. Among these, amidst all the murders that are committed, only around five thousand "Remo" are left. The people on the foothills refer to the "Remo" as animal. But the Bondo tribals know themselves only as "Remo". In their language "Remo" means "human being". The educated folk living in the plains, why do they find the opposite meaning for everything concerning the Bondos? Has "Remo" in the form of man been born on Bondo hills as animal?

In the Bondo legal framework, killing a man is not a crime. Only when angered does one kill. It is entirely the fault of the one who causes anger. The attacker is not so much to be blamed. For a man-killer, there is no jail, only a fine. According to laws, a cow or a buffalo, cooked rice, some 'sapung' (wine) is to be provided for all the kinsfolk of the village. All hard feelings with the dead Bondo's kinsfolk are resolved. That is enough to cleanse the man-killer off all his sins. Out of the thirty-two villages in Bondo-land, such a feast is organized in one village or the other every eight to ten days. These feasts never fail to make the village folk happy. The dead man's family members also eat in the feast. That's what the law decrees in Bondo-land. But the legal machinery of the civilized townsfolk ensures the imprisonment of a man-killer for ten to fifteen years in the Koraput Jail. After being released, yet again, a feast is organized in the village. The man-killer washes himself clean in the silver-gold water, and later drinks that water. The tribe accepts him back. But by the time a Bondo returns from the jail, there is nothing left to call his own. By then, someone or the other has by force acquired his property, wife, cattle, plough, salap tree, anything and everything that had belonged to him. But then, he can ask his wife to touch salt, soil, cow dung, the tiger's tail and to solemnly promise not to get married elsewhere during his tenure in jail. If this is done, she would truly wait for him, for fourteen or fifteen years. Yes, his wife will be there for him, but no property. Those who have power, have land. The wife would be there, no doubt, but what about her age? Gosh – a complete oldie, haggard.

When the Bondo youth is around seven to eight years, he starts courting girls. The girl would be around twenty to twenty-two years; in an ideal marriage, the bride should be at least ten to twelve years older to the groom. Bondo law prohibits marriage if this condition is not met. After fourteen years in jail, eating rice and curry, the Bondo youth would come back, strong and brave and the now ageing Bondo woman would be faithfully waiting for him. But it is not so easy for the Bondo man to divorce his old, unattractive wife and set up house again. This time round, the bride-price would be double. The Bondo becomes old once he crosses fourteen. The Bondo women wouldn't easily agree to get married to him. There is no marriage without the consent of the Bondo woman. One can however run off with a partner. Even in that there are lot many problems at times, even murder. If the girl had been forced into marriage, then even after setting up house, she had the liberty to be free from her husband and marry elsewhere. For this, though, the second husband was required to pay double the original amount as bride-price. Some Bondos would even agree to pay this stipulated amount for some other Bondo's legally wedded and willing wife. A Bondo is never reluctant to exhibit and prove his masculinity. He would pledge his land and cattle and would provide his services to his kinsfolk as bonded labour. Only then, and after the payment of the bride-price can he take someone's wife to be his own.

When Buda Kirsani left for jail, he had everything, his young wife "Sunki Toki", land at a high altitude, watered land, spade, axe, a pet dog "Kalia", and four hens. How old was Buda Kirsani then? He was yet to grow a moustache and beard, probably fourteen or fifteen years. Buda Kirsani had killed his own father, but it was the father's fault, of course. Buda had no fault, he had committed no crime. For every Bondo, there is his own Salap tree.

A salap wine tree is planted in the name of each and every Bondo man, at his birth. When it is around fifteen years old, the tree provides juice. In order to be proclaimed as a youth, the Bondo is required to break the pot atop the tree and drink its juice. The Bondo youth drinks a great deal of the Salap wine juice, raises a family and his harvest is rich. By then, the father along with his tree gets old. The old tree becomes incapable of yielding sufficient juice. The father begins to eye the son's healthy tree. Stealthily, choosing the most appropriate moment, he steals the pot collecting juice and drinks from it. Will any Bondo ever tolerate this? Even if the Bondo happens to be the son, stealing someone's wine is like having an illicit relationship with another's wife. Among the Bondos, when a young Bondo girl marries, her father-in-law is still quite young. The father-in-law takes great care of the daughter-in-law secretly, in the witching hour of the night, away from prying eyes. The Bondo youth, quite naturally, suspects the father, doubts the elder brother. A venomous snake bares its fangs in him. If he chances to see anything, he strikes. If, on a quiet, lonely afternoon, the son spots the father rushing out of the daughter-in-law's room, then the son strikes to kill, instantly. Once, in an isolated hour of the afternoon, seeing his father enjoying a cozy tete-a-tete with his wife, Buda had struck him immediately with an arrow. But the spirit of the ancestors had changed the direction of Buda's arrow and made it aimless. Father narrowly escaped that time. Yet another day, in the sleepy hours of the morning, Buda spied his father attempting to bring down the pot of wine from his very own tree. Without giving it a second thought, Buda shot an arrow from where he stood. The arrow found its mark, and Buda's father along with the pot fell to the ground. The juice from the broken pot wet the ground, and along with it, the dark blood from his father's chest. His father's life flew away. That day Buda Kirsani didn't mourn or cry for his father. Buda directly went to the police and said, "Arrest me. I have killed a man." Buda didn't have even the slightest trace of remorse, for he knew he had punished the guilty; whether the latter was his father or his son, made no difference. When Buda left for jail, his wife was all alone at home. When Buda was eight years old, he married the twenty-two year old Sunki Toki. After three years, Sunki gave birth to a beautiful baby boy. Buda was around eleven or twelve years then. Isn't Sunki's son Buda's son too? After all Sunki is Buda's wife. The son was two years old when, once, Sunki was working in the mountain slope, leaving her sleeping son under a tree. A stone flew in from God-knows-where and split open the bee's hive. It fell to the ground, and the wild bees stung the child from head to toe. The child was swollen up like a log and without uttering a single word, fell into a death sleep. Buda himself performed the last rites of the child. In this agony, he was gloomy for one whole day. Yet he did not shed a single tear. The Bondo man is very hard-hearted, aggressive and uncertain - doesn't easily give vent to his tears. That is why the educated mass refers to them as animals. But do the educated folk ever understand the gains and losses of the Bondos?

When Buda Kirsani went to the jail, he had everything; when he returned, he had nothing. No property, wife, house, plough, spade nothing. Mangla Badnaik of the neighbouring village had seized everything. Sunki Toki had deserted him and set up house with Mangla Badnaik. Sunki Toki is not to be blamed, though. Buda had never made her promise, as was customary in Bondoland, to wait till her convict-husband returned from jail. So why would she hopelessly wait and in the course become an old woman? But why did Mangla seize his property, wealth, everything? Who would ask him? In Bondoland, land or house is not registered in anyone's name in the government record. Anybody could burn the forest, cut the trees and cultivate (slash and burn cultivation) whenever he wanted. Whenever one chose to cultivate, that piece of land, the tree everything came into his possession, automatically. Mangla Badnaik has now been cultivating Buda Kirsani's land for the last fourteen years. So the land is rightfully his. So is the salap wine tree growing in that piece of land?

With the aid of his unfailing muscle-power, Buda could have got back his land, his wife. But it really is not that easy. Because Buda hasn't returned from the jail as a muscle-man; he has returned, diseased and ailing. The medicines provided in the jail were not good enough to combat the diseases. In the jail, who would perform the rituals to propitiate the deities to cure him of his diseases?

Buda's Bondo mind was aflame with an intense desire to avenge him but his fast disappearing strength didn't even permit him an attempt to kill. Most of the jail-returned Bondos are orphans, like him. Those who return strong and stout from the jail either kill and go back to the jail or get back their land and wife. The diseased Buda Kirsani saw red, no doubt. But his anger was in vain. Mangala Badnaik explained to the Panchayat that he had not forced Sunki Toki to set up home with him. She had come with him of her own free will. So he was willing to pay the 'bride-price'. This was okayed by the Panchayat. Mangala Badnaik, in lieu of bride-price, provided a pair of cows, two baskets of cooked rice and two rupees to Buda. The Bondo law now recognized Sunki Toki as Mangala Badnaik's wife. With the money he got, Buda threw a feast for the Panchayat and his kinsmen and was accepted back. The mistake he had committed of having interacted with the thieves and robbers of the town in the jail was now forgotten.

Buda found work as a bonded labourer of the money-lender, an affluent person of the village. This is the best, most profitable alternative for the landless. He would work in the money-lender's land. Twice a day, he would be provided with rice-water, some wine, too. The fear of hunger won't be there. At least he will survive.

The money-lender, however, was initially quite reluctant to accept Buda's proffered services. Bondos are very insincere at work. The women are hardworking. They would toil in the money-lender's land with unadulterated sincerity, as though it were their own. This is precisely why the money-lender preferred women workers. As for the men, they are lazy in their own fields, lazier still in the money-lender's. Of course, the money-lender in Bondo-land is unfailingly a Bondo. No non-Bondo money-lender s can be found in the Bondo Hills. Whoever has the privilege of owning three to four extra salap wine trees is labeled as "money-lender" in Bondo Hills. A salap wine tree is worth much more than a man's head.

And Buda is mere man; lazy and jail-returned on top of that, a diseased wreck, so much more insincere at work. But if he is not given the job, how would he live? No land, no hillside slope to cultivate, no wife. So 'Soru' of Buda Kirsani's own village, accepted Buda's service as a bonded labourer. If Buda would be insincere at work, the 'money-lender' would be insincere in providing him food. This was the crystal clear understanding. No one would utter even a word.

The bonded labourer would slog the whole day in the money-lender's land. At night, he would sleep in his own house – if his wife would be with him. If not, he would sleep at the dormitory for young, if his age would be appropriate. But Buda neither had wife, nor age, not even his own house. He slept anywhere he could. However, just alongside the ruins of his former house, he has raised another roof. Primarily because, a young salap wine tree was making elaborate plans to luxuriously blossom there. He had planted that tree before leaving for jail. This was Buda's wealth, he needed no more. Mangala couldn't take the tree along to his village.

The day freshly jail-returned Buda was shocked into stupor at the sight of his broken-down house, was shocked into sitting down with his cheek in his hand, he was stunned by a whimpering sound at his back. Is anyone crying? Is it Buda's mother's spirit?

In times of misfortune, the spirits provide support to the Bondo. Buda glanced back. A dirty brown puppy was lying all alone. No mother to lick it affectionately. The villagers reported that Buda's pet 'Kalia' refused to go to the other village with Sunki Toki. It stayed back, guarding Buda's plot of land. It became old, haggard as time went by, mothered many puppies. All strayed away. This one was the last. After giving birth to this one, old 'Kalia' passed away. It has been eight days now. The village folk have been feeding the puppy with rice-water to ensure its survival. The other two puppies died with their mother.

Buda pulled the little bundle of brown to his lap. He felt that he had a relative, who had been faithfully guarding his plot of land. Kalia is now dead but she has left behind her spirit in Buda's plot of land, to protect it. The day Buda had left for his exile in the jail, only his pet 'Kalia' ran all the way till the 'Bondo wall' (earmarking the limits of Bondoland) behind the police jeep. Everyone else stayed back at the outskirts of the village. His mother's spirit and Kalia's puppy are still waiting for him. What worry can ail Buda now? He lovingly named the puppy 'Kabra' because it was brown in colour. With Buda's careful and constant care Kabra survived. Kabra roamed around with Buda like his inseparable shadow. The four year old Kabra is huge and healthy. What is Buda feeding him? He is himself not getting enough rice-water to satiate his hunger. How could Kabra look so prosperous?

Is it the power of black magic? Kabra would not leave Buda even for a split second.

Buda ploughs the money-lender's land and Kabra keeps walking behind him. Otherwise, he would stay near the boundary, his face nestling on the front two legs, joined together to form a cushion, staring unblinkingly at Buda. In whichever direction Buda would move his plough, Kabra's innocent, sparkling eyes would meander; as though it was Kabra, not Buda, who was ploughing the field. The money-lender doesn't feed Buda well. In Bondo Hills, eating well means having a swollen tummy to bear testimony. Of course viewed this way, there would be very few Bondos who would have a swollen tummy to show off, all through the year. Just as, irrespective of the amount consumed, the dog's tummy shrinks back to its spine, so is it with the Bondos, no matter how much wine they drink. So, if the money-lender is not providing Buda with satisfactory meals, it's more Buda's fault than the money-lender. Buda would have roamed around aimlessly, like an orphan. Money-lender has been generous. Moreover, following the mutually-agreed-upon-rule, Buda's food is in keeping with the work done.

Buda never shares his rice-water with Kabra. In Bondo Hills, almost every house has a pet dog. But dogs don't have rice-water, only the excreta of man and pig. Licking the juice of rotten fruits in utter delight, they shadow their masters faithfully. The dog barks when it picks up the scent of a tiger. It grows ominously when it recognizes the stealthy steps of the wolf. If a snake slithers over a bed of dry leaves, the tell-tale leaves snapping under its weight, the dog rushes after its prey like quicksilver. From the manner of barking, a Bondo knows where and what danger is lurking. Kabra never demands food from Buda. It searches and relishes worms and excreta, and satisfies its hunger. Kabra is Buda's pet only because, it knows from the very smell and feel of Buda, that it is truly loved. That is why it has unquestioningly, voluntarily accepted Buda as its master.

Buda finds Kabra very beautiful. No human kid on Bondo Hills can be as beautiful as his very own Kabra. A Bondo child is so sickly, hands and legs like sticks, a pumpkin of stomach sticking out, eyes swimming in mucus, the whole body marked with rashes and skin diseases and an ever-running nose. They don't take their bath, don't brush their teeth, and don't wash themselves clean of excreta. Even the elders are like that. They will sit, eat, sleep, and ease themselves anywhere and everywhere. They will pick up almost anything and eat it. Chicks, piglets, puppies all move around with their mother. The mothers would nurse them, pet them, and make them feel cared for. The Bondo children move around on their own, borrowing, searching to eat. Cow-dung, stones, wood, pebbles are their most favorite toys. They would splash around in muddy puddles, pig excreta, liberally pasting the fascinating mixture on their own selves, petting themselves in childish delight. The animal kid would be licked clean by its mother. The mother of Bondo kids would be slogging in the fields, working in the forests, gathering food. The father would be dead drunk, would be killing and spending life in his own, unpredictable manner.

The mother gives birth to the child. The father shares absolutely no responsibility. And why should he? A Bondo child has no concern for its father. A Bondo man only desires the life of his child that his child should live. How he would live is God's problem, not the father's. Though Kabra is a true dirty-brown, it is beautiful, roly-poly. Not sickly at all. Face covered with fluff, just like a bear's. Two fan-like ears-dropping downwards. A little sound and they straighten up like a peacock lifting its tail. Not a very long body with thick legs, Kabra's prized possession is his long, plump tail. When a dog has such a tail, it indicates an aristocratic clan, a potential to be an obedient pet. Not a cut-throat traitor like man. When there is time, Buda always remembers to fondly caress Kabra's tail. At the touch of Buda's finger, Kabra takes great pride in swelling up its tail and making it appear thicker still. Once in every fifteen days or month, Buda measures the circle of Kabra's tail, holding it in his palm, whether it is getting longer or shorter. Kabra gets his soft ears pulled as if the tail is not found to be any longer or perhaps a fake slap on his hollow cheeks. Kabra then knows that he is being punished for some crime, but what that is, is beyond his comprehension. He wags his tail in a placating manner; with his legs resting on Buda's shoulder, Kabra licks Buda's face. If in a drunken state, Buda would occasionally respond by licking Kabra's fluffy face. He would hold Kabra in a tight embrace and roll over. Like a human kid, Kabra would hide his face in Buda's broad chest, blinking vigorously. He would try to be enveloped in the warmth of Buda's affection.

Lot of people has been eyeing Kabra. The Project Officer of the Bondo Development Agency offered an enormous, unheard of amount of fifty rupees to Buda for Kabra. Buda was not greedy about money; he was greedy about Kabra. Barik Dom was telling that an officer in the Block Office at the foothills was interested to buy Kabra. He was willing to pay around sixty rupees. Buda chased Barik Dom with a raised arrow. Buda embraced Kabra and said, "I will never sell you off, my Kabra. If I ever do that, I promise I will eat your shit to atone for my sins. If anyone else takes you away, the tiger shall take me, this I solemnly promise." Kabra, as though comprehending everything, blinked his eyes and wagged his tail in agreement. The two ears stood up straight, to attentively listen to the master. With Kabra, Buda Kirsani comfortably spent his days on the Bondo Hills.

It has been many days now since Buda has relished any non-vegetarian dish. But then, is the money-lender expected to feed Buda with crab, fish, and dried fish? If he would roast a chicken, would he offer a piece to Buda? There is no Sahukar who would feed his bonded labourers with fish or mutton. No prey was available on the hills these days. The slash and burn cultivation had shaved clean the once densely forested hills. The animals Bondos liked to eat were almost extinct, though the tigers and bears feeding on the Bondos were still around. Mutton or fish had become a dream on the Bondo Hills. In times of festivals, the entire village gets together for 'Biru'. There would be a piece of beef for everyone. Without a festival, without the worship, it is no longer possible to have mutton.

For the last two to four days, Buda Kirsani has been

absconding from the work in the money-lender's fields and intensely searching for a prey in the jungle. Not even a crow or a bird to be seen. He is tired of looking for the rabbit, mongoose, and snake. He did chase a snake with his vigilant arrows across three hill slopes. The snake got the better of him ultimately and dashed into a hole. Kabra raged around. But the snake did not reappear. Worms, which are popular delicacies with the Bondos would not be available these days. He was longing to savour the now-forgotten, mouth-watering taste of 'paste of ants'. But where are the ants? Have they all disappeared from the hills? A hopeless Buda returned to his only solace, the salap wine tree. He drank to his fill from the pot. Then he went to work on the money lender's slope, Kabra following him faithfully.

Kabra too is totally useless. Not fit for any kind of work, he can't even get hold of a mouse. The flesh of the mouse is silky, soft, and very tasty. Buda's drunken, dry tongue instantly watered. Without working, Buda simply sat down, fascinated by all possible meat flavours in the whole wide, world, tasting his imaginary recipes and feeling happy. But he was not contented; rather the desire to taste meat became even stronger. He kept sitting and ruminating about a possible alternative, but there was only darkness everywhere, nothing else.

The night was alive with few days left for the festival; seven to eight more days to go. Only then will the festival be celebrated. All kinds of new vegetables of the seasons, along with meat would be boiled together. Everyone will eat. But Buda was no longer prepared to wait for eight whole days.

As the seconds became minutes, the night became darker still. Buda's drunken stupor deepened, the longing for the taste of meat became uncontrollable. Buda Kirsani, in his intense yearning, grabbed hold of Kabra. Who else is there, barring Kabra, to share his sorrow in this Bondo village of man-killers? Kabra wound himself around Buda's chest and closed his eyes in the warmth of Buda's affection.

An emotional Kabra's ears were erect, when Buda's lips happened to touch them. The cotton-soft touch of Kabra's ears was like yummy mouse-dumpling. Buda dug his face into Kabra's ears and drew in a deep breath, right into his tummy – the smell of meat. The flesh of mouse, dog or cow - everything seemed similar. There is no distinction of flesh, of blood. Kabra's plump tail seemed like a snake to Buda's touch. Snake flesh is very sweet.

The devil in Buda raised its ugly head, the flesh-hungry ghost. He sat up. Opening the only piece of cloth he was wearing, he tied Kabra's mouth tightly. Kabra didn't protest. He wondered at this novel display of affection by his master. Even in intense intoxication, there is still a human living in Buda. Buda mused, "He would have flesh, by hook or by crook, that very day. Is he to be deprived of this pleasure only because he is a bonded labourer? Aren't bonded labourers men too? If the government has elaborate rules for exiling the murderer in jail, then why isn't the stealer of his land, wife and cattle not arrested? Isn't he punishable?

Despite the anger, hunger, drunkenness and hostility, the 'human" in Buda gave constant reminders, "Of course, you will have your fill of flesh. But your dog won't die. Let it live, you can still satisfy your hunger. Think about some way'.

Man is not a dud – he is very cunning – extremely clever. With a swift swish of blades Buda cut off both Kabra's ears. And then, the thick tail was severed right from its roots. From deep within the recesses of Kabra's tied moth, an agonizing whine emanated. In helpless surrender, Kabra, minus his ears and tail, wound himself around his master. Buda now untied Kabra's mouth. The ferocious knife in Buda's hand scared Kabra no end. He understood, then that his own master had attacked him. For self-protection, in the twinkling of an eye, he disappeared into the mysterious light and shade of the jungle.

In his ecstasy at the prospect of tasting Kabra's ears and tail, the joy of tasting flesh at long-last, Buda went into a euphoric dance. He lit a fire by rubbing two stones. He roasted Kabra's ears and tail, and then enjoyed it, all alone. Not in any way inferior to mouse flesh, sweeter than snake-flesh. After the meal of Kabra's tail, Buda drank some more and went into a deep, contented sleep on the slopes.

It was dawn when Buda woke up, and called, "K-a-b-r-a, Tch, Tch." No response. Buda, all of a sudden, got back his senses. He ran all the way to the project office like a man possessed. The project officer was having his customary morning tea. A few other workers were chatting with him. Buda squatted in front of the officer and let out a heart-rending cry.

The officer was stunned. Buda was an orphan, no wife or children, no land; so what misfortune could have come Buda's way? Had he killed again? Was he mourning his return to the confines of the jail?

The officer asked – "Are you drunk?"
- "No, No."
- "Have you killed someone?"
- "Oh no."
- "Then what crime have you committed?"
- "A great crime. Arrest me. Beat me up. Punish me."
Buda pleaded.
The officer questioned him – "Then what have you done?"
- "My pet dog, Kabra…"
- "What happened? The tiger got him?"
- "No-No."
- "Then? Have you sold it off to satisfy your hunger? You didn't give it to me. How much did you sell it for?"

Buda's eye turned blood-red. He circled around ominously. With his bow and arrow ready, he said, "Don't you dare talk in that manner, or I will kill you. You might regard the Bondo man as an animal, but he never sells his pet."

The officer gave an involuntary start and moved away from the arrow. In a placating tone, he continued – "I know how much you care for your Kabra, you can never sell him. But where is your Kabra? He guards you like your shadow…"

Buda beat his breast and howled, "I ate him. In my longing for flesh, I cut off and roasted his ears and tail and ate it. Whenever you want to have meat, you can have your wish. But from where will a bonded labourer get flesh? In my desperation for having flesh, I lost my senses. Kabra has left me and gone. I am orphaned.

Kabra will not even cast a glance my way…" Buda's tears, sobs, repentance were springing from within his soul. There was absolutely no doubt that Buda loved Kabra very dearly, even more than his own life. He hadn't cared so much for his father, son or wife. Buda didn't shed even a single tear after killing his father, didn't cry when he lost his only son. Buda was not in the least bit saddened when his wife deserted him for someone else. But now, his eyes were raining tears, such tears as no Bondo has ever shed. It was so surprising. Bondo kills man at the drop of a hat and such repentance for merely cutting off a dog's ears! Along with the officer, the group assembled there burst into peals of laughter till they could no longer do so. They failed to understand Buda's agony. Buda was nonplused at the mirth of the townsfolk. He was thinking, "How can these people not understand such a great calamity? And they call the Bondos animals?"

Buda cried even more that no one understood his sorrow. There was no one to feel for him, stand by him on Bondo hills. Only Kabra had been there, Buda started beating his breast anew.

Buda felt someone resting on his shoulder. A very loving, very familiar face was nestling near Buda's. Someone familiarly touched his ears and licked it tenderly. Buda turned round. Embracing the ear-cut, tail-cut Kabra, Buda cried piteously, repeating constantly – "My Kabra." The townsfolk laughed even more at Kabra's strange appearance and Buda's unbelievable animal-love.

Poor Kabra is an animal – a wild one at that. It is beyond him to understand so much. He was only licking the tears, wetting his wild master's face, assessing Buda's affection from his salty tears. Had it not been for his animal birth, he could have interpreted the meaning underlying his master's tears, which was beyond the comprehension of civilized townsfolk.

The Untouchable God

Translated by **Sachidanand Mohanty**

How prim and proper were our beginnings when unclothed and unmindful, men could roam freely! How secure and generous was the age when without shelter, society and civilization, man lived innocent at heart – a complete denizen of the wild!

If this civilization and society could be destroyed within the flicker of moment, then man could once again turn wild, become a perfect beast. Then he would not have to stretch his hands out to others to clothe his body. He would not eye others daily – out of shame and unease. Everywhere there would be unclad beings like him. People would not be looking at others out of hunger, hatred, ridicule or embarrassment. The fact was, however, that everyone barring herself wore dresses, petticoats and blouses. Now even her last cloth had become fragile and worn out. She had forgotten its origin and the number of years it had lasted her. The old rag clung to her body like her own skin. While bathing in the open, she could not remove her dress.

She was forced to take a dip with the dress on. And as her body dried, so did the dress, all by itself.

It is hard to recall the original colour of the cloth or whether it has designs of fruits or flowers, leaves or stars or shapes of diamonds. She was busy keeping herself alive and had no time to think over such things. In the mingling of time and her struggle, the colour of her skin and dress had turned into one dirty brown. However, while it lasted, it was the sole source of her pride. She did not know then that not just food but even a piece of rag could infuse life into man, circulate blood in his capillaries.

The day that torn rag dropped from her body, like the shell of a dry sore, she, completely nude before herself, wondered how she would survive. How she would live, she thought. How could she carry on life with her unclad self? She felt as though her life were departing from her limbs. The veins of her forehead throbbed with anxiety. Her ribcage vibrated with a deep sense of unease. Her throat dried up with shame and insult. If only her skin rather than her cloth had fallen; what was the good of the cover that did not protect man from the elements or shame? If only a kind-hearted money lender would come by. Perhaps he could remove his skin and exchange it for an old rag. Should she end her life then, she wondered.

Much before she was conscious, some monster seemed to have cut out a morsel of his flesh, rather a piece of liver, and put it on her lap. She did not know who the father of her child was. A handful of rice was the cause of her nemesis. Before she could quench her hunger, the devil had satisfied his own. While her stomach was satisfied for half the day, the hunger of two stomachs had opened its mouth from that very day. She did not know what joy that nether region had given her; all she knew was a terrible pain. When awaiting the hunger of the whole world, she realized that some disease was raging deep within her. When the unknown scourge ravaged her adolescent self and came out in the open, she knew that very day that she had become a mother. Strangely enough, it was the disease inside her that had kept her alive for so long. How could she hope to die by casting her liver into the fire of hunger or continue with her nude self in the open marketplace?

For two days she hid her face by turning her back to the town and the village. Like a patch of tar on a dirty track, the piece of flesh clung to her milk less chest and sucked her life blood. After all, how much blood did her heart contain? Like a severed centipede, the morsel of flesh hanging from her chest writhed in pain. Inside her stomach too, there raged a fire of hunger. The fire offered no illumination in the midst of enveloping darkness!

She did not know when exactly she came and stood near the main bazaar in her naked self for a handful of rice. Someone was grinning at her, another turned away his face in disgust, and a third caught her eye. As for her, she seemed totally oblivious of them all. She was crying repeatedly only for rice. Only to quench the hunger of her stomach!

Looking at her unclad body, people exclaimed: "The bitch' not an old hag but a youthful woman, that's what she really is! See, the people give her rice but none offers a cloth. A nice pretext she has for her livelihood!" True enough, the crowd drove her out, and none threw a rag to cover her. She knew that even those that turned away their faces out of shame, those very people from the corner of their eyes did not refrain from relishing her nakedness. It was as though her body was special, different from others, as if her naked self-contained something more than a fully clothed one. From small to big, everyone stared at her wide-eyed. They abused her on the ground that in the thoroughfare of polite society, she was sowing the germs of obscenity. But it seemed to her that more than her own nudity, their naked language was far more obscene. Yet there was no way she could protest. After all, she was not begging for the respect of society, she was only pleading for rice. Who but her knew that to her rice was more important than clothes!

Initially of course, she had felt a sense of shame. She sensed as though everyone's gaze, pierced her body. Despite her outstretched hand, no voice came out from her throat. She wondered about the wisdom of this world where one person wore clothes, another went naked, one ate and another went hungry. Right from her childhood, she had been on the road. She did not know who her parents were. Like her, there were so many who were born and died on the road. Even cows and cattle, dogs and cats were needed by society, by man. But who needed the two-legged beings of the wayside: they were unwanted and homeless orphans? Could her society be other than the human one? In her nomadic society of beggars, no one bothered about dress. Why was so much fuss made over one person's nudity?

Parting her hair into two strands in the middle, she drew them in front and spread them upon her open chest. Her aim was to use these to cover her shame. In God's creation, there may be hunger without food, growth of the body without cloth and luxuriant hair without oil. How amazingly neutral God can be! She was half relieved now; for she was able to cover the shame of at least half her body. Now she might even come across a donor. But what was this? Spotting her disheveled hair, people exclaimed: "Look at the mad woman!" Urchins threw stones. On all sides, the crowd teased, pestered and finally angered her. After all, there was a limit to the human patience! She lost her cool. To ward off the hail of stones, she clenched her firsts and went on a biting spree. This would be the best way to tame people, she thought; as a kindled rocket, they would not dash after her. But the result was just the reverse. Now she was taken to be a confirmed lunatic! People avoided her sight lest the "mad woman" did something rash. Who knows what wild brain wave she might nurture! Now she was absolutely relieved. After all, what was shame to a mad woman! She had already lost her sense. She set out detached, fearless, and unclad. Perhaps she had truly become God, she thought.

Unlike food and sleep, a sense of shame is not a congenital habit with human beings. May the Lord Almighty be praised! Difference, after all, is only a matter of habit. Still, habits can be given up. Thus, her desire for garbed self, like a passing cloud, gradually shrunk and finally disappeared. She now strode along without fear. It was all for the good, she thought. Her headache over, henceforth she could ask for rice instead of clothes. With this, she resolved that her life would be on the right track. There was no more worry. Perhaps it would be better for the whole tribe of beggars to discard all clothing and roam around naked. That way there would be less pressure on the donors. How much more could they be expected to give! It would be mutually beneficial if some of the demands got reduced.

The naked self seldom bothered about the weather. The skull of the poor man served as his umbrella, his skin was the bulwark against rain. Nevertheless, the biting cold penetrated through nails, teeth and tears, not to mention the bone marrow. Like straw pulled from a thatched roof, the cruel winter sucked flesh from our skeleton. Without a torn rag, the mother and child could hardly hope to survive against the piercing cold of winter. In the wild, man may not have had clothes, but at least he had the bark of trees. If not a home, at least he had the caves of a hill for shelter! She, of-course, had no clothes to cover her body. How then could she face such terrible cold?

Yet, why should anyone give clothes to a mad woman? Was she a God or Goddess that if someone was to give her a piece of thread, it would make her blessings turn into a boon?

Leaning against the outer wall of the temple, the "mad woman" made a vain attempt to put up with the cold. She envied and cursed the many gods and goddesses. Why did God give her a human form, she wondered. If she had a body of wood and stone, she would not have asked for clothes or rice yet she would have become immortal. There is no counting the sarees that donors piled upon a deity. Their cost amounted to thousands and thousands of rupees. Pata, Matha, Banarasi, there were so many types of sarees! The eyes of the "mad woman" dilated in disbelief as she eyed the sarees offered at the altar.

And yet, her entreaties to donors to part with an old rag always fell on deaf ears. After all, what good could be there in giving away a saree to a vagabond woman? It was the priests who appropriated them after wrapping them ceremonially around the deity. That's all! Only once did the deity accept the saree as part of the ritual observance. Aside from that, the deity wore nothing else. God alone knew the fate of the pile of sarees. But she never tried to solve that mystery with any priests. Who knows, they might have exploded and showered her with choicest curses. How dare the mere picker of leaves aspire to bargain over the price of a mango grove, they might have wondered.

Clutching her body, the mad woman lay prostrate before the entrance to the temple, thronged by devotees. If only some would part with a piece of cloth or a morsel of food! After all, there were regular offerings made at the altar. Not just platefuls but successive rounds of food! It seemed that the fragrance of the offerings quenched the hunger of the Lord. The very same fragrance pricked the hunger of the mad woman too, inflaming her empty stomach. She had the urge to collect a little morsel in her outstretched hand, and shove it into her tummy. But try as she did, her hands could not stretch far enough.

Didn't the Lord himself accept offerings with outstretched hands, she thought. Wasn't he called the one with the longest hands? If he had no hunger, then why did the devotees pile a heap of good at his altar? What good did it do to deny an empty stomach for the sake of a hungry God? Should she ask the priests to explain this mystery to her, she wondered. But perhaps it was better she did not bother herself with such weighty questions. After all, wasn't she a mere picker of leaves? Daily she saw and smelled so much food. That should be enough! Even a dead baby got up at the smell of the offerings. Even a rickety child got a fresh lease of life. The smell of food should be more than enough, she thought.

Outside the temple, the mad woman daily witnessed the play of God. But, was it really God's play or rather the play of man, she often wondered. After all, God did nothing, all seemed to be man's handiwork.

The God of wood or stone did not need any food, dresses, flowers, sandal-wood paste or incense. If a mere block of wood and stone could turn into the Almighty by the worship of flowers and sandal-wood paste, then daily on the altar or the temple, the speakers could all put on garlands and become veritable gods.

But he who presided over our destiny, could he be oblivious of the fact that he was least interested in garlands and offerings? What did he need of dresses, fragrances and offerings?

Whenever the biting cold or hunger became acute, the "mad woman" offered only this prayer: "God, make me like you, only a block of wood or stone. I shall never ask for rice or cloth any longer. Like you, I wish to smile at the illusion of the world, sitting immobile like a block of wood!"

That day mounds of offerings were literally burnt before her very eyes. No one knew why so much food became so mysteriously impure. Such a thing never happened. No wonder the priests had to bury all the food meant for human beings, courses and courses of regular offerings. Like colour, like smell! With the same food, the life-line of both, the mother and the child, got extended.

Why did an offering ever become impure? And if it did, then what prevented God from partaking from it? In that case, at least the "mad woman" and her child could have had their fill. However, who was she to open her mouth before the laws of the temple! A mere woman of unknown caste!

What, by the way, was her caste? Was she a Brahmin or an untouchable? What was her religion? Was she Hindu, Muslim or something else? Only God would know, "the mad woman" knew nothing.

She only knew this much that she recognized no difference of caste or clan. Nor did she bother over cold or heat, old age or death, caste or clan.

Who could have erected the barriers of caste, clan or religion, she wondered. Wasn't man himself the God? How blissful was the time when man had no other affiliation. She could not approach God simply because she had no caste and clan. Or else, she could bury her naked self in the dark cavern behind the altar, repose within the precincts of the temple and save herself from the rain or dew. If nothing else, she could at least hug the deity and pour out her grief.

That day, the child who usually clung to the mad woman's

chest like a leech, somehow escaped and with tiny steps toddled into the precincts of the temple. Her mother's exhausted self-had slumped outside. It was a perfect scandal, a real calamity.

Loads and loads of offerings were being carried for the lord. With tiny hands outstretched and saliva dripping from the mouth, the child pleaded: "Rice, please give me some rice'". The priests were unmoved. The deity was totally immobile. "Finished! It's all over" they said in chorus, "The god-forsaken child has entered inside the temple 'All has become grossly impure. What a terrible tragedy!

By then the priests had circled around the child. Seeing their forbidding figures, wide eyes and fiery gaze, the child swallowed his saliva mixed with tears. Thank God, as an untouchable's offspring, he would not be handled by the priests. They could not crush his flesh and bone. The milkman, who carried water for the Lord, covered his nose with a piece of cloth, lifted the child by one arm, and with a grimace dumped him outside.

In an instant the tiredness of the exhausted mother vanished. The child continued his ceaseless chanting: "Give, give, give me rice'" The lord stood mute and immobile. If God could become impure by the presence of an ignorant child within the temple premises, then was the temple meant only for a barren woman?

No, the temple had to be purified. At the odd hour, the deity was given a ritual bath and made pure. So much hassle and expense! The mad woman did not have a roof or hearth. Otherwise people would not have hesitated to extract compensation from her. The woman thought and thought: How could the Lord ever become an impure being, an untouchable? Was he not the true Lord? Was he only a wooden puppet or an idol of brass! He who purified all the dross of the universe, turned sin into merits, who could make him impure? Could the impure ever become pure by the human touch?

She sought an understanding to the hidden mysteries. But one who had no food inside her, no cloth over her back, how could she have thoughts in her brain? Perhaps that was a sensible way of looking at things!

If the destitute had no worry, then they would not have had sorrow. The tragedy of the mad woman was that she thought more than she was supposed to. For years, she had been lying near the temple, hearing the preaching in the holy scriptures, the Shastras and Puranas, from pundits, monks and gurus. She had understood one thing: All that the Shastras and Puranas preached was not necessarily true. In fact, she had discovered the very opposite of what she had been hearing all along.

Now that the temple offerings and the deity were threatened with impurity, she recalled the story of Neela Madhava in the house of Sabara. There were other parallels too, Dasia Bauri and Salabega. He whose invocation lessened sins, how could he ever become an untouchable?

One who had no caste or clan, could be ever be a sinner? And one, who called God by a single name, could she be an enemy of religion? The mad woman became confused. Before whom could she express her thoughts? Even if she were to do so, who would listen to her and reply? If thoughts had no value, then why did God create a web of them? It must have been only to increase the quota of sorrow! Holding the child close to her chest, the mad woman sat once again as dumb. She saw the passage of hordes of devotees, saints and sages. She had seen them everywhere: in houses, markets, shops, offices and other places in the world. And she saw them in the temple too. Here, their face and eyes looked different. The dress and appearance were of a different kind. People offered so much to the lord: crowns of gold, sarees and thousands of rupees in the donation box. Even without God's asking, there was an increase in donation inside the temple. Yet none had given her so far a single paisa, a morsel of rice or even a piece of torn cloth! Whoever had given had parted with reluctance and ridicule. Once inside a temple, men tended to put on a new mask, just like painted actors in the play of Ramalila. Well, she had never gone inside temple. How could she know the glory of God? If only she could enter even once, perhaps then, like a latter-day Karna, she could part with her child. There would be one worry less! She could then be at the mercy of God. She could not fathom whether it was God or man who was untouchable. God could very well be untouchable! After all man was never prohibited from touching God. It was only God who seemed averse to human contact. God communicated and lived through the priests, holy saints and kings!

The mad woman had a great desire to talk to God. But there seemed to be no way to do it.

Today the cold bit and hurt like the sharp thorns of the cactus plant as the women lay covering her child with one arm. She knew she could willingly bear the cold and the hail stones and offer comforting warmth to her child. The devotees all looked plump in their winter wear. The woman was simply amazed! How could they even breathe with such heavy layers of dresses? Could there ever be many clothes in the world! Even the smallest piece was enough to save her from the cold. Perhaps then, she could have made a perfect fool of the weather! But who would understand this!

The cold engulfed all, like mighty flood waters. Even snuggling inside her mother, the child shivered. If only the mother's life-span could be converted into a blanket for her child, then perhaps her life would be worth it! Yet longevity was always a worse enemy than poverty. It always had the upper hand!

From outside, the woman looked at the special costume of the Lord who looked like a real prince. Matching his dress was a garland extending right down to his feet.

There were so many costumes and appearances of God that her eyes had seen from far. Different costumes matching different offerings. There were so many people, constantly on their feet for the upkeep of God! Yet how was it that they never looked tired, weak or diseased? If anything, they seemed to maintain better health than God. This must be the result of the "spiritual" service they were rendering! Perhaps the task of living did not require any emotions. Perhaps the hunger of the stomach was all there was to life. Perhaps the bigger the stomach, the narrower was the heart! Otherwise, one's life span was bound to get shortened.

The mad woman was hunger personified. How large her

heart had become, thanks to a surfeit of sorrow! If only she had belonged to the upper caste, she could have washed the vessels of the Lord and widened her girth as well as the girth of her child. There was a cushion on the altar of the Lord to ward off cold. The velvet cover as well as the silk blanket-all had been changed. The Lord rested in his nocturnal costume. Did the Lord truly go to sleep? Lies, all lies! She thought. The Lord, she surmised could never sleep. He was always awake. His bed and blankets were always fresh and clean. It did not look as though anyone had slept there.

Did the Lord ever look sleepy-eyed! Every day, he had the same world-piercing gaze. Did it mean that he always got up early, arranged his own bed and sat on the altar?

It was now time for the Lord to rest. The doors of the temple closed firmly. The front yard became deserted due to the intense cold. In this world, even the bird had a nest for its beak, a branch to perch on and the sky for its flights. And yet, despite being a human, the mad woman had no home of her own. She was even less than a bird. Clutching her child to her chest, she dragged herself down to the temple doors. From the ledge, a stretch of the ceiling was seen. Perhaps she could find a little warmth beneath it. God and birds – all craved the warmth within. Only she and the stray dogs could not. Hadn't God given the dog a winter dress of fur? Why then had God created man inferior to the dog? Was she truly a human? If not, then he could have at least given her the life of a dog? In her sticky hands, the woman held her half-dead child close to her bony chest. If only the child could break open his mother's rib cage and get into her heart! Then perhaps he could be spared from the cold. But alas, that was not to be. It was not easy for the human heart to break open-even if it be for one's own son!

The sickly child grew increasingly dulled by the cold hand of his mother. The woman called out once: "Oh Lord, please save my child". Then she allowed her frozen body to slump down.

The human self may be closed to one's fellow-men but the sky remained open to all. Now it spread blanket upon blankets of mist over the mother and the child. Then the two of them fell asleep forever. Blissfully! There was no more cold or pain for them!

The next day, at sunrise, people saw the dead bodies at the portals of the temple. It was as though the woman had placed her head on the threshold in a spirit of everlasting prayer! As every day, the Lord was found on his seat. His bed and blankets seemed intact. It was business as usual!

Did the Lord ever retire? Was he ever affected by cold, hail, heat or rain? Like him, even the mad woman was now above the elements; wasn't there any difference between the two? Was God a human person and was man truly God? Perhaps such talk carried no meaning.

There was brisk action within the temple to purify God. Preparation was soon afoot for the ritual bath of the Lord. What a punishment to God even on a cold day! However, the Lord remained unfazed. Sitting on the altar, the idols were all smiles! It was hard to make out who was foolish- man or God! The fact was, dead bodies at the threshold of the temple simply meant impurity. The temple had become impure! And there was impurity everywhere!

The mad woman too was smiling at God. There was a flicker from the corner of her lips. Her laughter was heard by none other than God. As for humans, they could only see the stale corpse of the dead woman, with her hideous and frightening looks.

Transgression

Translated by **Bikram K. Das**

L ying on his dead-bed, Bhabanath remembered
his life's companion, Savitri. Forty years had
passed since she left him. Would he find her waiting
on the other side? Did people really wait for their
partners after they had crossed over? Man and wife
were supposed to be companions for the entire cycle
of births; even so, what would Savitri gain by
waiting for such a worthless husband? Who could
blame her if she deserted him?

How old would she have been now if she had
survived? Bhabanath wasn't sure. But she would
surely have been strong enough to take care of him.
No matter how much neglect she suffered, she would
never have left him to die unattended. Eight years
after their marriage, when their son Srinath was
only five, she was snatched away by some unknown
disease. True, he had not spent his days in loving
contemplation of her face, but how could he have
known that she would be as short-lived as the gourd
flower? Shortly thereafter, Sarala, their three-year
old daughter, passed away. They almost lost Srinath

too, but the child had clung tenaciously to life. Bhabanath was young then, but he turned down every proposal for a second marriage. And now Manju, wife to the same Srinath, had abandoned the seventy-year old hulk and walked out of the home to her father's house. Srinath was away in some distant place, tied down to an unrelenting job that would not allow him even a day by his father's bedside. That was every serving man's fate, not Srinath's alone. You did not own the head on your shoulders; it was pawned to another. On the one hand, you desired the clink of silver coins and, on the other, the freedom to return home each month; but how could you have both? Still, Srinath did manage to come home occasionally and whisper into his wife's ear that the old man was not to be neglected. If Manju neglected her God-like father-in-law, she would be consigned to hell; casual acquaintances as well as relatives had recited this endless litany in her ears. Was a father-in-law any different from a father? Wouldn't Manju have taken care of the dying man if he had been her own father?

She had dedicated heart and soul to his service. From her first day in this family she had pampered the old man as she would her own child, wiping away thirty-five years of loneliness with her devotion. People who observed her remarked "She must have been his mother in an earlier birth. Bhabanath felt the same way, and he blessed her from the depths of his heart. His one prayer was that he might be allowed to go painlessly. The longer he lingered, the more Manju would suffer.

Before he was bed-ridden he would sit hunch-backed on the verandah, leaning against a wall, and stare fixedly at Manju. There wasn't even a kitten in the house so that he could have turned his gaze to some other object. He had never known how much pleasure there was in gazing at a daughter or daughter-in-law. That was because he had never looked directly at Savitri in eight years of married life, never seen her face in clear daylight. It was always midnight when she came to the bedroom, after she had attended to all the duties of a full household. The oil lamp had burnt low and it was pitch dark. Besides, what interest did he have then in gazing into Savitri's face?

Bhabanath was respected throughout the village. He never raised his eyes to stare at the daughters or daughters-in-law of the village. Even as a young man he spent most of his time in the the family shrine, poring over the scriptures, his forehead marked with the deity's sacred symbols. He was practically a saint, coming home only at his mother's insistence. On most days he would take some of the food that had been offered to the deity, and stretch out on a straw mat on the verandah of the village temple which was an extension of the family home. The elders used the place for the chanting of prayers but the young men assembled elsewhere, for His praises were sung in ten neighbouring villages.

It was natural for the fathers of eligible daughters to desire him for a son-in-law. Their daughters would be fortunate to marry such a pious young man, of such lofty character. They would bring forth worthy children. What more could one want? Unmarried girls offered champak flowers to Lord Shiva, praying that the god would bring about their union with Bhabanath. Savitri must have attracted the envy of other girls of her own age when she married Bhabanath; but what did she get? The poor girl never knew what a husband's affection was. He had never gazed in wonder at her face, never whispered words of love into her ear. Eight years she spent behind the veil. By God's grace she became pregnant and Srinath was born. Her existence as a woman was crowned; the family name would endure. Life was complete.

Was Savitri's life really complete? Why did she cross death's threshold when Srinath was only five? What strange sickness made her wither away? Bhabanath could not tell. His parents were there to look after her, while the village doctor   treated her illness. Bhabanath was not by her side during her last moments. How could he be so shameless as to sit on his young wife's bed, in the presence of elders? It mattered little that she was dying. Of course, he yearned to caress her fading cheeks, to bathe her forehead with tears. But the restraint of manhood prevailed over the lover's tenderness. Dignity had to be preserved. Besides, what benefit was there in attachment to a mere lump of clay? It was only human weakness that made one cling to worldly attraction, even in the knowledge that everything was illusion. But Bhabanath had put weakness aside. Savitri's body was carried out of the courtyard in procession, the beat of drums announcing that she had died in the blessed state of wedlock. No one ever saw Bhabanath weep. This was manly courage indeed! Those who had come to comfort him had to be comforted instead. "It makes me sad to see you grieving for me. Why mourn? She was blessed. She has been spared the pains of this illusory world. As for Srinath, why feel sorry for him? He who has provided the shade of a mother's love will surely look after the child. The parents who give birth are mere instruments." Everyone marveled. Those who had come to sigh and commiserate returned with his praise on their lips.

Women had reason to envy Savitri's death. The years that she lived were glorified by her husband's fame. She had become the mother of a son, never known sorrow or suffering. The veil over her head, which was the banner of wifehood, had remained in place; her body had never lost its youth. The vermillion in the parting of her hair glowed brightly on the funeral pyre, proclaiming a woman's ultimate privilege of dying in matrimony. Could one have a happier life, a more splendid death?

Who could say that Bhabanath was an unworthy husband? What faults did he have? Was he dishonest, a debauch, a wife-beater? Had he ever given Savitri cause to complain? Yes, she might have grumbled that he was unromantic. To which the reply would have been: "For shame! Isn't there such a thing as decorum? How did you become a mother then? Did you expect him to give up his devotions and dance by your side all day? There were family traditions to be guarded ."

But Savitri never faced such questions, for her tongue had never uttered a complaint against her husband. Her home had lacked nothing, it was a full, loving household. If something had remained unfulfilled even then, the fault would have been hers.

Bhabanath remembered everything as he lay on his death-bed. His dull, lifeless eyes could see clearly what the bright eyes of his youth had failed to see.

Who had ruled that it was sin to look at a woman? Who had decreed that looking at one's own wife with desire was lust? Who had proclaimed that youth must reject passion and craving of the material world and turn its thoughts to the spirit? Who had created these embankments that separated virtue from sin, good from evil?

If it was sin to look at a woman, could a man earn virtue by blinding his own eyes? What sin was there in proclaiming beauty as beauty? The goddess Laxmi was beautiful, Durga was vivacious, Saraswati silver-voiced. Didn't everyone proclaim this loudly? Was that sin? It was to shield himself against such a sin that Bhabanath had made himself senile in his youth. He did not regret it. He had grown old in devotion to the family god. But no one had seen him look at the daughter or daughter-in-law of another. No one had seen the symptoms of lust arise in his mind. He had got married at the insistence of his parents, only to protect the lineage. It had been a duty. But in his thoughts he had remained celibate. Would he have retained his strength of mind if Savitri had lived on? He could not answer with certainty. Was it for this reason that Savitri appeared again and again to his dying eyes? Those glimpses were as faint, as fleeting, as the touch of the stealthy winds of spring.

What did Savitri look like? Her sharp-featured face, seen through the long veil of her sari - red, blue, purple or multi-hued like the clouds - was like the soft glow of the lamp lit on the deity's altar at evening. Her fresh body, draped in the sari, was like the sprig of sacred basil offered to the god. The tender feet, dyed scarlet with alta, were like rangoli patterns painted on the floor. The two arms, covered with auspicious gold bracelets, were like half-woven wreaths of multi-coloured flowers, the palms of her hands were like lotus petals strewn on the god's image, the slender fingers like the sticks of sandalwood used to create sandalwood paste for the god. The crimson spot of vermilion on her forehead was the risen sun breaking through the dark clouds of her hair; her gold nose-stud was the morning star. Was there room here for lust? Fragrance arose from her hair like clouds of sacred incense;

her breath carried the odour of a lamp that had glowed brightly on the altar and then extinguished itself, fulfilled. Everything about her reminded him of the rituals of worship. There was nobody here, only emotion. She was the image on the altar. This had been his relationship with Savitri after Srinath was born. Could one call it neglect?

No one had accused him of being a bad husband-certainly not Savitri. Yet he found himself, for some unknown reason, defending his own conduct.

God knows what might have happened if he had taken to feasting his eyes on the daughters and daughters-in-law of the village after Savitri's death. But he had covered his eyes with a blindfold. Eyes crave beauty, and beauty generates lust. That was why Bhabanath had kept beauty at arm's length and why the world respected him for his character. When the first mango blossom appears, the cuckoo breaks into song; with the corning of spring, branches grow heavy with clusters of flowers. In the first flush of youth, the buds of desire burgeon; the abandon of the cuckoo's song echoes in each mind; nerves grow taut with excitement. No one gives birth knowingly to such feelings; they happen of themselves, like the change of seasons. Is it a sin for a flower to bloom? Is the cuckoo's song a crime? Then why is society opposed to the truth of the seasons? Today it appeared as though everything was a sham, a camouflage for the evil within. The moon looks bright because its other side cannot be seen. The other side of the mind is hidden too, and so the earth seems virtuous. In his youth Bhabanath had been inspired by the Vedantic philosophy of "The world is false, and the Infinite is the only reality." The world is transient; its flavours are poisonous. This world is not our permanent home; therefore, clinging to the world as "mine" is a delusion. The Infinite could be gained only when every bond of attachment was severed; it was this belief that had led Bhabanath to lead a life of detachment in the midst of worldly activity. But there was not even a glimpse of the Infinite, let alone the promised union with the Infinite. Was it self-deceit then to say the world was false? Bhabanath's family deity was Jagannath,

Lord of the World. If the world was false, how could its Lord and Master be true? Such questions rose often in his mind, but he turned away from them in self-condemnation. In other words, the world was false, but the Lord of the World was truth. If the one Infinite could appear throughout the false world in so many different guises, was it not an insult to the Infinite to call the world, to call life, false and to focus on union with the Invisible, the Intangible as the only goal? This mortal, fallible world is the path to the Infinite. Then, why try to prove that it is illusion? Both life and death are subject to the laws of mortality. Why then had Bhabanath rejected the gifts that life could bestow and aspired to attainments that could only follow death; why had he played hide-and-seek with life and truth? He had treated his virtuous wife as though she was a temptress, rejected love and romance as though they were forces of destruction. Yes, he had earned great respect for his piety, but had he attained salvation? Why did the Infinite elude him still? If death was the avenue to the Infinite, then why, in this hour of deliverance, did the temptress Savitri return again and again to haunt his memory? Bhabanath had always honoured Bhishma, the conqueror of desire, over Kamadev, the God of Desire. He had made Bhishma his ideal and led a life of celibacy after fathering a progeny, in obedience to his own father. Why was he so anxious now for union with Savitri in the world beyond, when he had disdained union in this world? Was the hope of spiritual union another form of self-deception?

On his death-bed Bhabanath thought of the birth that he was about to forfeit. He had always considered renunciation greater than indulgence. Yet here he was, concerned about the cremation of his own flesh. Who knew if he would be born again in human form? Did re-incarnation really exist?

He had rejected the entire female species, not just Savitri, as illusion. He had never been a father to his daughter. No wonder she had departed early! Bhabanath had not looked at his own sister after she attained youth. He could not remember if he had looked his own mother in the face.

But Manju, ever since her marriage into this family, had

been more than a daughter. He could not believe that he had been capable of so much affection. He had thought of himself as a dry log. What sap could it contain? After his daughter-in-law arrived, Srinath refused to let him live in the temple and forced him to come back to their home. The old man had survived on a handful of food, cooked by the old Brahmin priest. But the Brahmin's son had no interest in the temple. He would hurriedly prepare some rice and half-cooked curry and rush off. Then, high on puffs of marijuana, he would wander away to the village club-house. Now, for the part of his life that remained, Bhabanath would eat what his daughter-in-law cooked and be looked after by her. In his younger days Bhabanath had turned down a similar command from his father, but he could not refuse his son. He packed his bundles and came back home. The temple gaped at him wide-mouthed, like an orphan child.

The temple's thatch had not been repaired for some time. The sun and rain, seeping through the canopy that covered the deity, bathed it without fail. The mud walls had not been plastered. The thought of scooping out the old well, which had got silted up, had not occurred to anyone. No one was prepared to take the responsibility of the daily temple rituals. The god could look after himself!

Bhabanath bowed to the deity and told himself "Let your wish prevail, Lord! I had rejected my father's wish but could not say no to my son. I have been an unworthy father, a stranger to love and affection. Let the happiness of my son and his wife comfort my last days."

Bhabanath was devout, strong-willed and unattached. He had been thirty-five when Srinath's mother died. Many proposals had been received but he had never even considered a second marriage, afraid that a step-mother would ill-treat Srinath. He had never looked at another woman. The temple was his whole world. He came of an aristocratic, high-caste family. Keeping a concubine while one had a wife was considered a sign of aristocratic living. Bhabanath's younger brother had maintained three concubines. No one would have said a word if Bhabanath had taken a concubine, but he had no such despicable inclination. A string of sacred basil beads round his neck, the mark of Vishnu on his nose, prayer beads in hand; a short dhoti, barely concealing his knees, a crude waistcoat round his chest, in winter, a rough shawl across his shoulder and in summer, a long scarf on which the hundred names of God had been printed. Hair growing like paddy stubble, tied into a single top-knot. Half-closed, detached eyes, constantly engaged in counting prayer beads, prominent nose, robust physique, swarthy, slightly bent at the waist, the effect of humility, not age. It is said that Narada, the supreme devotee of Vishnu and a life-long celibate, had acquired eternal youth. Bhabanath was not to be compared with the great sage, but he might have resembled other renowned devotees such as Dhruva or Prahlad in their old age. As he sat cross-legged on the front verandah in the devotional lotus posture, eyes closed, passing men and women bowed low in reverence. To Srinath he was the living image of Jagannath, their patron god. His devotion to his father was unshakeable. "The father is dharma, he is heaven, he is the ultimate destiny." Srinath was respected in five neighbouring villages for being Bhabanath's son. What other achievement did he have? On the first night following his wedding, he had whispered no words of love into Manju's ears; instead, it was the recitation of his father's greatness that took up the entire night. He had clearly told Manju that to him his father had precedence over everyone, including her. Even unintended neglect would not be forgiven. If his father was happy Srinath would be pleased. Srinath had always held his own mother guilty of deserting his father in his youth. From the first day, the new bride Manju knew that this house rested on foundations of service, not love.

No one was unaware of Manju's devotion to her father-in-law. It was this quality that had won Srinath's heart, rather than her beauty or her love for her husband.

Whenever Bhabanath looked at Manju he was reminded of his own daughter, who had deceived him and left. If she had lived she would now have brightened some home, just as Manju was doing. Then he remembered his wife, Savitri. How proud she would have been of such a daughter-in-law! But the poor woman could never know what happiness was.

Manju gave her full attention and care to Bhabanath, as though he was an infant. She thought of him as her aged son, not her father-in-law. And Bhabanath, on his part, was constantly nagging her with his anxiety about her welfare. "Eat well; dress well; laugh and be merry; take care of your own health. Why is your hair so dry? Is the house short of hair-oil? Why are you looking glum? Reminded of your parents? Look, I am here, your old father!"

At times Srinath felt envious of the love Manju was getting from his father. He had never received so much attention himself. He would tell her, laughing "How lucky you are! It is a wonder that such an unattached person can give you so much love! I don't remember getting even half the love that he has given you. But of course, such a good daughter-in-law deserves what you are getting! If you had neglected him, he would have been back to the temple by now,"

Manju's face would light up with satisfaction. Srinath, who had been transferred, went to his new posting, assured that his father would be well looked after. Any other wife would have insisted on accompanying her husband. Which daughter-in-law would agree, in this day and age, to stay back in the village to nurse an aged father-in-law?

Srinath left. Bhabanath was unhappy when he heard of his son's transfer. But strangely, he felt relieved too. Some unknown feeling of expectation rose within him. Now Manju would be entirely his daughter-in-law. All her time would be devoted to him. There would be no Srinath to claim a share.

These days, when a girl referred to her family, it was to her husband, her children and herself. That was all. The aged had no place there. But in this regard Bhabanath was fortunate. And Manju was fortunate too. Which father-in-law treats his son's wife as his own daughter? Bhabanath's affection made the pain of separation from her husband bearable. When Srinath's letters came, they were mostly lists of things she had to do for his father;

there might be a line at the end for her. Sometimes she resented being ignored, but the next moment she felt that by giving his father priority over her, Srinath was displaying his humaneness, not his weakness. She felt doubly blessed in her husband and father-in-law.

At first, Manju would veil her face with the tail-end of her sari when in the presence of her father-in-law. Her face, seen through the veil, seemed to him to resemble Savitri's face. "You needn't cover your face," he would tell Manju, "You are my daughter, aren't you?" Manju's veil would often slip off her head. The thick knot of her plaited hair, the smooth neck beneath the knot, the necklace of gold beads around the neck-all reminiscent of Savitri. Into that necklace had been woven the history of the family, its honour and self-respect. Since some unknown time the necklace had passed from mother-in-law to daughter-in-law, generation after generation. Bhabanath's mother had passed it on to Savitri. When Savitri died, some relative rescued the necklace from her neck before she was cremated and handed it over to Bhabanath, saying "Keep this safely. If Srinath grows up to be man, you should give it to his wife." Bhabanath put the necklace away in an old trunk and it was presented to Srinath's bride when her face was first unveiled to her new relatives. It was a beautiful piece of jewellery. Each gold piece was followed by a coral bead. Strung on a black thread, with a gold pendant in the middle. It would look good on any woman's neck. But Bhabanath had never had occasion to admire it on Savitri's neck. That afternoon Manju sat resting on the back verandah. An irresponsible gust of wind tugged her veil away, revealing the nape of her neck and a portion of her back. Half of the bead necklace was seen, glistening against her skin. Below the necklace were two black moles on Manju's fair back. How pretty! What was pretty? The gold necklace or the golden neck? Or the black moles on Manju's back? Bhabanath felt as though it was Savitri sitting with her back turned to him in complaint. Was there a mole on Savitri's back? He couldn't tell. Why did Manju remind him of Savitri repeatedly? When Manju turned her head, she almost died of shame to find her father-in-law staring at her exposed back. How could she have been so unmindful!

Now Bhabanath seemed to be depending on Manju for every little thing. Throughout the day it was "Manju, get me some water; grind some sandal paste for me; make a garland for the god; bring me my prayer beads; get my puja things ready!" His requirements were unending. She would have to be hovering around him all day like a honey-bee. Still, Manju was loud in her praises of the old man. Not even her father could have been more loving!

But how long could she remain in the village to look after him? Srinath was finding it difficult to manage alone at his place of work.

If Bhabanath agreed, they could all go there and live together. Manju had proposed this to Srinath, who was of the same mind. But Bhabanath was upset when he heard of it. How could he leave his village and his gods in the evening of life? If either Manju or Srinath was inconvenienced on his account, she could go away with Srinath. He would not interfere. But he would not go anywhere. Srinath gave Manju a scolding because it was she who had made him suggest something so improper to his father. All destruction has its origin in a woman's brain! His father must have thought that Srinath was so taken up with his wife that he could not live apart from her! How shameful! "Stop worrying about me," he admonished Manju. "I am young and strong enough to manage. But can he? Never think of leaving the village as long as he is alive."

Manju felt guilty and said nothing. Yes, she had created an unseemly situation. Her father-in-law would think she couldn't bear to be separated from her husband, that she was tired of looking after him. If she served him devotedly she would be blessed, and Srinath would get the fruits of her devotion. She would never do anything henceforth to hurt the old man's feelings.

Manju never spoke of leaving the village again. She had now begun to massage her father-in-law's legs. It was Srinath's wish. Who else was there to soothe his tired limbs? When Srinath was at home he would massage his father's body. Now it was Manju's turn. She found it awkward at first, but gradually lost her hesitation. Was a father-in-law different from a father?

Bhabanath enjoyed the touch of Manju's soft fingers on his legs. This was how Savitri had massaged him at night. It was as if Manju had snatched away the two hands of Savitri! One night Bhabanath sat up with a jerk while Manju was massaging his legs, as though he had seen a ghost. Glaring at Manju like a jungle cat, he gripped her small hands in his. Breathlessly he said "Your mother-in-law's hands were exactly like yours, Manju! That's why I love your massaging!"

Manju eased her hands out of his grip. Without a word she left the room. She sat alone in the room next to the kitchen, where the rice was husked, thinking of all manner of things. God knows what message she read in the old man's eyes or in the grip of his hands, but now her own house seemed eager to devour her! Some unknown fear was planted in her heart. Her father-in-law no longer appeared to be a god. He was a mere man, a stranger. But she could not reveal her mind to Srinath or to anyone else. Besides, who would believe her? She would be blamed instead. "All that the old man did was to remember his wife and look what a fuss she is making! The evil is in her mind."

But no language is needed to read a man's heart. A woman's eyes are like a touchstone. She can tell from a man's gaze, from his touch, even his breathing, just how much gold and how much dross his heart contains. Now Manju could look vividly into the old man's heart. When gold is firm, it conceals all dross, but when it melts the dross is exposed. Bhabanath had no control over himself now; he was melting. He needed assistance for each activity-sitting, getting up, going to the toilet, bathing, eating. Srinath kept on reminding Manju "Take care of him. If he falls and breaks a limb at this age, that will be the end." But Manju could not always manage alone. When she called the servant Dama for help her father-in-law got irritated. Dama was a low-caste untouchable; his touch would defile. On at least two occasions the old man almost fell in a heap on top of Manju. While she struggled to regain her balance he grabbed her to keep his decrepitude intact. Dama rushed to help, only to be scolded by Bhabanath. These repeated incidents were like poison to Manju. She wrote to her husband "I am unable to manage Father alone. He needs my help at every step, but I am not strong enough. He narrowly missed a fall more than once. Please come home at once; I need your help."

And his answer was: "Do you think I would have left him in your care if I could get leave to come home? Besides, if I do come home for a day or two, of what use will it be? You have looked after Father for so long; what made you write such a letter at this stage of his life? I hope you won't do it again."

All doors were closed for Manju. Who could she narrate her doubts to? Anyone who heard her story would condemn her. She could never tell Srinath "Look, your father is a mere man, not a god!" The words would remain unspoken, out of fear and shame. One night she had felt the stealthy touch of a groping hand. "Who is it?" She screamed, sitting up with a start.

"It's only me," said a low voice, "Why are you afraid, Manju?"

"What are you doing in my room at this hour, Father?" she asked. "I thought you were unable to walk without help, even in the day-time. How did you come here by yourself?"

"I wanted to go to the toilet," the old man replied. "I didn't feel like troubling you. But I must have lost my way in the dark. I can't see clearly."

"You should have shouted for me, "Manju said anxiously. "What if you had fallen?"

"I would have been killed, I suppose. I don't want to live on and be a bother to everyone." There was infinite regret in the old man's voice. By the time she struck a match and lit the oil-lamp, he had staggered back to his own room and bolted the room from within. Hadn't he felt the urge to visit the toilet? Then why was he hiding his face inside the room?

More than anger or hatred for her father-in-law, Manju experienced a sense of helplessness. He was far older and more frail in body than her, but the respect he commanded had made him taller than the Himalayas. She could not, even if the occasion demanded it, raise her hand to strike him or push him aside and step over him; she could not even talk to her husband about him. Who could she tell about the transgression of that sacred relationship? Who would believe her? In someone younger it might have been explained away as the momentary excitement of youth; but how could such conduct be reconciled with the respect and honour that should accompany old age? Manju felt feverish and nauseous all day. It was as if all the polluted winds of the earth were blowing into her face. Even the deities seemed to have lost their sanctity when she sat down to her ritual worship.

To her husband she wrote: "Come before it is too late. I am no longer strong enough to look after Father. He is becoming difficult to manage. If you delay any longer, I shall leave him in the care of the servant, Dama, and go away to our own home. I can't carry on..."

He could have come at once, but Manju's letter bore a threat which he could not stomach. He spent the next few days sulking. Meanwhile, Manju slept with her door unfastened, lest she should be unable to hear the old man's call for assistance in the night. She was unable to sleep. Towards midnight, when she was beginning to feel drowsy, she felt his groping hands once again. He seemed to be possessed by some evil spirit, determined to destroy all trust, morality, tradition.

But for Manju it was not possible to transgress the limits of self-respect, of ages of tradition. She could not tell her father-in-law, "Father, the eyes of God see even in the dark. There is hell..." How could she? What if her suspicions were false? What if he had really lost his way in the dark? When Manju screamed the single word, "Father!", he tottered out of the room nervously, like a dog that has been caught with its muzzle in the cooking-pot.

Manju stood confronting the dreadful ghost of her own suspicion. But as soon as night passed, she left for her father's home, abandoning duty, responsibility and tolerance. Veiling her head with the end of her sari, she bowed low to her father-in-law. Tears came into her eyes. Hardening her heart to the old man's helplessness, she climbed into the bullock-cart. The reproofs of the entire village decay, had revealed its hideous face!

Bhabanath could admit his sin to himself, but could he tell his son or daughter-in-law that such depravity was not entirely abnormal? It had overcome the sages Soubhari and Chyavana, the great King Dasarath, and many other elevated souls. He wished he could have begged Manju's forgiveness and resigned himself to death. But no, he could not look into that innocent face again. She had done well to leave. Who could trust that demon?

He felt grateful to Manju and blessed her in his mind. He could not look Srinath in the face, could not open his lips to say "Manju is not at fault; it is this barbarous old man who is to blame." And so his lips were sealed.

Srinath was heart-broken to see his father's plight, but anger at Manju's behaviour overshadowed all other feelings. Dama said "How the old master loved her! No one ever heard him speak a harsh word to her. How could she desert him in his last hours after all the care she had taken of him? She was more than a daughter!"

Bhabanath wanted to dispute what he was saying, to exonerate Manju of the unfair accusations of neglect. He wished he could have lashed his own back with a whip. But he was unable to do anything. His voice was stifled. Senility had made him powerless. Manju's tender face had turned fearsome, like that of the goddess Durga, the demon-slayer. The slightest agitation of the earth could bring down the civilization of aeons; so too, the least aberration of senility could tarnish the restraint and virtue of a lifetime. He silently cursed all those who had mistaken the detachment of his youth for saintliness. With a restless mind he prayed "God, give me back my youth. Return my Savitri to me. Restore my strength. I want to taste life as a normal human being; I have no desire to be a god. If all this is to be denied to me, God, punish me for my sin and take away my salvation. Let me be born again! Let me be born again!" The tongue that had chanted God's name for a lifetime fell silent while it was praying for re-birth.

Manju returned when she heard of her father-in-law's death. She stood over his dead body, shedding tears of guilt, but did not have the courage to touch those cold feet with her forehead in a last farewell. The bier was lifted out of the courtyard. No one had any sympathy for her; instead, she was condemned all around.

How many twigs and bits of straw float away unseen on time's current! Srinath and Manju were wholly absorbed in worldly matters, but Srinath's harsh, unforgiving gaze kept asking her one unspoken question: "Are you not guilty before God for the way you treated my father?" There was no answer from Manju, but her eyes revealed the burden of her guilt. How many histories of transgression were poured over her in a flood. Even the trees were commiserating the old man's plight, the servant, Dama, was angry. What a heartless woman! Leaving her home because she had an old wreck to look after! Did she have no fear of divine retribution?

When Srinath got the news he came at once. Since the day of Manju's departure, the old man had taken no food, surviving only on the sanctified water in which the Lord's feet had been bathed. Tears misted the comers of his half-shut eyes. He had forbidden Dama to touch him. He would not speak a word; he had turned into a block of stone. Looking up, he seemed to be contemplating the forms of the Death's messengers, who had surrounded him. Bhabanath was well-versed in the Vedas, but he was no rishi. If he had been a rishi, like the sages Soubhari or Chyavana, all his sins could have been forgiven. But he was a mere house-holder.

The scriptures were full of examples of venerable old rishis who, after a lifetime of celibacy, had chosen to wallow in the pleasures of the flesh. The great sage Soubhari, in ripe old age, had threatened to curse King Mandhata, of the Ikshyaku dynasty, unless he gave his daughter in marriage to him. Terrified, the king gave away not one but twenty-five of his daughters to the sage, who renewed his youth through his spiritual powers and enjoyed an abundance of connubial bliss. The rishi Chyavana had wedded

Princess Sukanya in his old age and prevailed upon the heavenly physicians to provide him with undying youth and virility. Ancient King Dasarath had married the youthful Kaikeyi. Kings too could be forgiven, but old Bhabanath? People compared him to a rishi, but could he find a young wife for himself by threatening to lay a curse on someone? To an ordinary person such as him, all avenues were closed. He had craved a woman's company before his son Srinath was married, but that yearning had been lacerated under the whip lash of his own reason and he had brought home a daughter-in-law instead. The sight of Manju's face had awakened, for the first time in his detached life, the flow of fatherly affection. No forbidden thoughts had ever tormented him. But why, in the hours before death, had that demonic passion peeped out of the looseness of his mind? He could not tell. The mere child that Manju was, younger than his own daughter. His son's wedded wife; his own daughter-in-law. Yet even she had caught a glimpse of the demon that lurked in the darkness within. Even if no one else knew, Bhabanath knew, and so did Manju, that he was no rishi. Oh God! How long that demon had lain asleep! When it could have been devouring human flesh, at the peak of its powers, it had chosen to subsist on food offered to the gods; but now, when bone and flesh were inscribed in the experience of the mature Manju! And yet, she had abandoned her father-in-law, who had been like a father, on his deathbed, unable to put up with a slight straying of his mind. Her tolerance could have made his last hours more bearable!

Each year, when Manju observed her father-in-law's death anniversary and made her ritual offerings to the departed soul, she told herself that the offering would not be accepted, for it was she who had transgressed. If those feet standing at death's door had stumbled, could she not steady them with her strong hands? Was Manju to blame? Whom could she ask?

■

About the Translators....

Jayanta Mahapatra, is an award winning Indian English author who has written around twenty-seven volumes of poetry. In 1981 Jayanta Mahapatra won the Sahitya Akademi award for his book "Relationships". He is a recipient of the Jacob Glatstein memorial award conferred by Poetry magazine, Chicago and was awarded the Allen Tate Poetry Prize, 2009 from The Sewanee Review, United States. He received the SAARC Literary Award, New Delhi, 2009 and an honorary doctorate by Ravenshaw University in 2009. He was also awarded D. Lit. degree by Utkal University, Odisha in 2006.

Bikram K.Das, is a well-known translator and a former Professor at the Central Institute of English and Foreign Languages, Hyderabad, and the National University of Singapore. He has to his credit several important English translations from Odia, including Gopinath Mohanty's Paraja, for which he received the Sahitya Akademi Award and Pratibha Ray's Adibhumi.

Sachidananda Mohanty is Adjunct Professor in the   School of Liberal Arts and Human Sciences. He was formerly Professor and Head, Department of English, University of Hyderabad and Vice Chancellor of the Central University of Odisha. He received the Katha Award for outstanding translation (1992), the Katha British Council Translation Prize (1994) and UGC's Career Award (1994-97). Besides two books on D.H.Lawrence, his essays and articles have appeared in some of the leading journals and periodicals in the country, including India Today, the Hindu, the Indian Express, Span, the IIC Quarterly, PEN and New Quest.

Kamalakanta Mohapatra, has published a collection of short stories, *Palabhut* (1984) and a novella, *Photo* (1990). He has translated, together with his wife Leelawati Mohapatra, works of Fakirmohan Senapati, Kishori Charan Das, Jagannath Prasad Das and Laxmikanta Mohapatra into English and Jean-Paul Sartre, Isaac Bashevis Singer and Gabriel Garcia Marquez into Odia.

Leelawati Mohapatra, has published in the *Illustrated Weekly of India*, the *Statesman, Indian Literature, Indian Horizons, New Quest* and *Journal of South Asian Literature*. In addition to the translations she has done with her husband Kamalakanta Mohapatra into English and Odia, she has edited, with him, *The Macmillan Book of Short Poems*.

Sudhansu Mohanty has published, besides many translations, several essays and book reviews in the *Statesman*, the *Times of India*, the *Hindustan Times* and several other journals.

Aparna Satapathy has graduated in Psychology from Utkal University. She has taken up few translation projects.

www.ingramcontent.com/pod-product-compliance
Lightning Source LLC
Chambersburg PA
CBHW050137110726
47898CB00008B/2562